BLOODY FEATHERS

DEATH OF THE CARDINAL

A Kim Jansen Detective Novel – 3

BRUCE LEWIS

Black Rose Writing | Texas

ISBN: 978-1-68513-151-7
PUBLISHED BY BLACK ROSE WRITING
www.blackrosewriting.com

Printed in the United States of America
Suggested Retail Price (SRP) $19.95

Bloody Feathers is printed in Garamond

*As a planet-friendly publisher, Black Rose Writing does its best to eliminate unnecessary waste to reduce paper usage and energy costs, while never compromising the reading experience. As a result, the final word count vs. page count may not meet common expectations.

Dedicated to my wife, Gerry—in life and writing—better together.

SPECIAL THANKS

Author and life-long friend **David Haldane** (*Nazis and Nudists* and *Jenny on the Street*) for introducing me to Black Rose Writing.

Authors **Chris Patchell** (the *Lacey James Mysteries*), **Susan Clayton Goldner** (the Winston Radhauser Mysteries), and **Martha Pound Miller** (*Child of Fate Series)* for their guidance and moral support.

Black Rose Writing: Creator and Founder **Reagan Rothe**, Social Media Jedi **Chris Miller** for his book promotion ideas, Design Director **David King** for his amazing cover and book layout, Sales Director **Justin Weeks** for smoothing the book distribution process, and **Minna Rothe** for her behind-the-scenes marketing work on behalf of all Black Rose Writing Authors.

Jim Carmin, Librarian, Multnomah County Library, for his stewardship of the Central Library's John Wilson Collections, a treasure trove of rare books for public education.

Nancy Freeze, constant reader extraordinaire.

BLOODY FEATHERS

"The moment a bird was dead, no matter how beautiful it had been in life, the pleasure of possession became blunted for me."
–Naturalist John James Audubon

FOREWORD

The best crime thrillers never reveal too much too soon. It's a sacred pact between author and reader. But wouldn't you like to know what motivates the characters you'll be living with for hours or days of your life?

Would you be more likely to read a mystery if you knew the main characters' lives were guided by the same inner forces and conflicts that get you out of bed in the morning—or keep you awake at night? I think you would. So, here goes.

Heart Surgeon Jed Miller: wants to be an eagle among sparrows
Artist Lexi Miller: wants to defy her critics
Detective Kim Jansen: wants justice for the victims
Bookman Bruce McQuillan: wants a legacy
Daughter Meg McQuillan: wants out
Uncle Dan McQuillan: wants what's owed
Chief Detective Mark Larson: wants love
Rare Book Curator Marc Stanfield: wants to save his family
Vintner Colin Byrne: wants redemption
Veterinarian Jim Briggs: wants a new career
Rare book librarian Bill Bowman: wants recognition

Now you know. Will it help you solve the mystery? Will it make you race through the book to learn the ending, to find out if the characters achieved their dreams? I hope so.

Thanks for buying my book and taking the journey with me. Writing *Bloody Feathers* was so much fun, as was creating *Bloody Paws* and *Bloody Pages*, the first two books in the Kim Jansen Detective Series.

–Bruce Lewis, 2023

CHAPTER 1

The Accomplice

They held tight to the rickety railing as they descended the wood staircase into the basement of McQuillan's Books. Decades of damp air and moldy paper records—dating to the store's 1938 opening—pressed down on them. When they reached the bottom, they stopped to let their eyes adjust to the dimly lit space.

"Over here," said a cheerful Marc Stanfield, lunging toward a man-size steel safe in a dusty corner filled with cobwebs. He was like a kid on a beach discovering a pretend pirate chest. In the safe was supposed to be John James Audubon's *The Birds of America*, four volumes with life-size paintings of over 1,000 birds, many extinct. Their value: $12 million. The Holy Grail of 50 million American birders. And among the ten most expensive books in the world.

"I really appreciate your understanding," said Stanfield, former curator of the Portland Central Library's rare book room. "I know I'm reneging on our deal to sell Audubon's paintings. But, the idea of the rarest of rare books going to a millionaire's private collection is too much. So I'll admit to the theft." He was babbling. "I'll say it was all my idea. I'll go to jail, then try to make it up to my family when I'm released."

"Are you going to return our buyer's $100,000 down payment?"

"I can't," said Stanfield. "I've spent the money—some for living expenses and the rest to support my wife and daughter."

His accomplice said nothing, nodding somberly as if understanding.

Stanfield walked to the safe, turned on his cell phone flashlight, and began dialing the combination. After a half dozen turns, the whirring of the retracting locking pins was smothered by the basement's moistness. Finally, he pulled open the door.

The safe was empty.

"Oh, my god," said Stanfield, "Where are the books?"

Suddenly angry, his accomplice yelled, "What the hell did you do with them?"

Stanfield looked back into the safe as if they might magically reappear. When he turned around, an 18-shot American Ruger pistol was pressed to his forehead. Enough for one kill shot and a lot more.

"Get in the safe."

"I don't understand," said Stanfield. His face was a mask of bewilderment.

"You can step into the safe or I'll shoot you and drag your body into the safe. Do as I say. Now."

"What do you mean?" said Stanfield. "Why are you pointing that gun at me?"

"You want to return the books to the library, so you took them."

"No, I have no idea what happened to them. I'm as surprised as you are."

"I don't believe you. And I'm telling you one more time to back up and step into the safe."

"Don't do this," Stanfield pleaded, tears streaming down his cheeks.

"I'm going to close and lock the door and come back in an hour. That should be plenty of time to think about your family and the possibility of never seeing them again. Then, hopefully, you will have changed your mind about returning the books."

"I'll die in there," Stanfield said, his voice a squeak.

"The fear in your voice tells me I might convince you there is no going back on our deal. A deal is a deal. Before I close the door, I'm giving you one last chance to change your mind."

Stanfield began sobbing. "I took the books to save my family and my marriage. You know that. You've got to understand that giving them back is the right thing to do."

"It's never going to happen," the accomplice said, shoving Stanfield into the safe, his head smacking the metal back wall. With a twist of the door handle and spin of the dial, locking pins slid into place, creating an airtight seal. No one would hear Stanfield's screams or whimpers as he slowly suffocated, hopeful he would be rescued at the last moment.

CHAPTER 2

Jed

1

Jed Miller steered his car into the International Rose Test Garden parking lot in Portland's Washington Park. Tall spruce trees shaded the spot.

Jed climbed out and buttoned up his coat against the winter chill. He stood looking across the garden's dormant beds where 10,000 rose bushes create a blaze of color from late May through October. During the blooming season, tourists and locals swarm like bees. This morning, the landscape was still. Sixty miles distant, Mt. Hood, slopes white with snow, stood out in sharp relief against the clear blue sky. He looked at his watch and figured he had another 30 minutes before checking in downtown for the Christie's auction.

Jed placed his hands on his car's hood. The deep red paint was the color of blood. The engine's warmth was the same temperature as a beating heart in his hands. He closed his eyes and allowed his mind to transport him back 36 years. A few days before his 14th birthday, he had arrived in Dayton, Tennessee, to spend the summer with his Aunt Mildred and two dozen cousins. His 31-year-old widowed mother said he would see where she grew up and have the adventure of a lifetime. She was right.

Aunt Mildred handed him a Daisy Red Ryder BB Gun on his birthday. His mother's present to him. He grabbed the gun, held it high, and danced around. "I can't believe it," he said. "I've asked for one since I was five years old. Mom said not in the city, too dangerous."

"Never point it at anyone," his aunt warned. "And don't be shooting out any of my windows." She also told him to keep a lookout for poisonous

3

copperheads. Jed spent the day exploring her two acres of weedy yard, kicking the grass to scare away lurking snakes as he went. He found a discarded stove, a shed with no windows, a tire swing, bins of cans and bottles, and piles of wood—a target-rich environment for his 650-shot load. He was so engrossed in his mission to kill the plethora of inanimate objects that he missed lunch.

Nearing exhaustion from the hunt, Jed found himself in Aunt Mildred's front yard. A chorus of cicadas filled the air as he stood under a sprawling red oak. The 95-degree heat and humidity enveloped him like a winter quilt but not as soothing. Lightning bugs emerged with the approaching dusk. He created his own mini fireworks show with point-blanks shots at the tiny fireflies, splattering their glowing tails.

The sights and sounds were all foreign to his Southern California eyes, where girls in bikinis and the surf, rather than bugs, were the center of his attention. That was before he heard a continuous chirping from high in the tree branches above.

Jed looked up and saw a bright red bird. A lighter red beak poked out of a black face patch, accentuating a headdress of feathers jutting from the top of its head. He would learn later it was a male Northern Cardinal. He had never seen a thing of such beauty at home. Egrets, terns, and gulls at the beach, sure. They paled in comparison to the bird he watched darting among the dark green leaves.

Is that what Aunt Mildred called 'anyone' when she warned against pointing the rifle? Jed wondered. His arms ached from his hours of target practice, and the gun hung at his side.

The cardinal came into view, then disappeared, hopping from branch to branch, hiding momentarily in the foliage, then returning to a large limb in plain sight, 15 feet away. The bird's body faced forward, its chest a glowing red beacon. Was this a challenge?

Unsure if the cardinal was an approved target, Jed cocked the rifle, aimed, and waited. The cardinal didn't move. Instead, the bird continued to look at him, his head turning this way and that.

Jed was well within the gun's 30-foot range. Even if he hit the bird—it would be hard to miss this close—would it shake off the .177 caliber pellet, the size of a peppercorn, and continue its carefree day?

The cardinal moved to a higher branch, hopped from limb to limb, then settled back in Jed's gunsight. Should he fire? What would be the fun of shooting—maybe killing—one of the most beautiful animals he had ever seen?

Jed loosened and removed his aching, raw finger from the trigger, then lowered the gun. The cardinal was defiant, challenging Jed, daring him to fire. Again, Jed raised the gun and aimed. His finger jerked. He wasn't sure if it was an accident or if he wanted to make the shot and get it over with. Traveling 350 feet a second, the BB hit the bird in the chest, the feathers and skin no armor against the tiny metal bullet. It wobbled on the branch.

Jed looked closer to see if he had hit the cardinal or if it was doing a little dance, taunting him. Wings out, the bird spiraled to the ground. It stood for a moment, then fell over.

A wave of remorse washed over Jed. He dropped the gun and rushed to the bird. It was lying on its side, one eye winking weakly. He picked it up and felt the wetness coming from its feathers. A smear of blood covered his fingers.

Finally, the bird's eye closed, and the warm body went limp in Jed's hands. Panicked—and excited at the rush the shot gave him—he took the bird to the shed in the backyard. There he found a paring knife and cut through the bird's chest to probe for the BB. He desperately wanted to patch up the wound and bring it back to life. There was no beat. No life. Jed was a killer, and there would be no resurrection. Tears flowed. "I'm sorry," he said. "I didn't mean to kill you. You shouldn't have dared me."

In that moment of regret, sobbing and wiping his nose, he held the bird loosely in his hand and remembered something his mother had said when his father died. She reached into the coffin, touched dad's chest, and said, 'My heart to your heart. The heart and soul are one. Today, we are one.' Jed put his hand on the cardinal's chest and repeated his mother's chant.

2

Jed snapped out of his daydream. The encounter had shaped his life in ways he never imagined at age 14. He climbed into his car and headed downtown for the auction of James Audubon's *The Birds of America*.

Nearly every seat was filled when he stepped into the auction room at the Portman Hotel. Jed had reserved a seat early and was in the front row. Because of the value of Audubon's work, Christie's Auction House sent a team from New York to handle the sale. Surrounded by armed guards, the books were showcased in a private room for qualified bidders, like Jed, who could prove their ability to pay at least $5 million. Christie's had wanted the books shipped to New York. The anonymous owner, a wealthy Oregonian, said she would never trust a shipper to safely move the books 3,000 miles.

The bidders—hands and paddles in their laps—tried to appear relaxed. Some would be investing their own money, while most of his competitors represented wealthy American and foreign buyers. Many held cell phones, talking with bidders 10 time zones away.

A woman in a light gray suit and white blouse with a bow, her lush blond hair pulled back in a chignon, stepped up to the podium. She introduced herself as Sally Stillman, auctioneer. The bidders sat up straight.

"Today, Christie's is proud to offer the extraordinary four-volume compendium of avian art, *The Birds of America*. The proceeds will benefit the owner's charitable foundation. We trust you have read the material on Mr. Audubon, one of America's great naturalists."

Stillman didn't mention that Audubon owned slaves. Or that in 2021, when members of the Audubon Naturalist Society in New York learned about his history, they removed Audubon from the society's name.

Still, Jed thought, Audubon's paintings were genius—art in their purist form—alive and beautiful. Possessing Audubon's masterpiece would set Jed apart from the top one percent of the world's elite birders—people like Sweden's Claes-Goran Cederlund. Cederlund had amassed a life list—bird's observed or recorded—of an astounding 9,760 birds, nearly 90 percent of the World's bird species.

Jed thought of Cederlund as a falcon among birders, gobbling up birdwatching records. Cederlund's competitors raced around the globe—no expense spared —to surpass the Swede's achievement. It was a millionaire's folly. You needed money, time, and help to reach the top. In the birding world, owning the world's longest life list was like a climber reaching the peak of Mt. Everest.

They were birding fanatics, like Jed, whose own life list topped 8,000 after 20 years of birding.

Before he set his sights on *The Birds of America*, Jed sought the record for the most birds observed in one year. His only serious competitor was legendary birder, author and ornithologist Noah Strycker. Strycker traveled to 41 countries and all seven continents to set a world record by finding 6,042 species of birds (more than half of all birds on Earth) in one calendar year. Jed had started fast, recording 2,000 birds in four months, then dropped out when his father died, and he had to return home to settle the family estate.

Finally, Jed pushed away his birding flights of fancy and focused on the auction.

3

Sally Stillman tapped the gavel twice on the podium and opened the auction with a bid of $5 million. A bidding frenzy followed. The price moved higher quickly with $100,000 bid raises. There were 25 bidders at the start. By $6 million, 10 bidders remained. At $7 million, the competition had shrunk to five. Jed was among them.

A minute later, at $8 million, Jed's heart pounded as adrenalin flooded his body. He was battling a man on a cell phone at the back of the room. After each raise, the man would talk to the anonymous bidder, then raise his paddle. Jed knew previous copies had been sold at auction for $9.5 million and $10.2 million. Some art critics estimated the Portland copy would hit $12 million. Jed's phone vibrated. Finally, a note from his wife, Lexi, wishing him luck. Okay, he thought, this is it. Now or never.

At $9 million, Jed took a deep breath as his mind spun like a Las Vegas slot machine, calculating the odds, estimating the potential impact on his net worth—and his life. He crossed his fingers.

Between earnings, tech sector investments, and bird poaching proceeds, he put their combined wealth at $50 million. He would have to liquidate major stock holdings to generate the needed cash. Tax consequences would be ugly. He had considered this before signing up for the auction. Still, he couldn't stay away. Now, reality began to sink in and his stomach clenched when bidding closed in on a final number. Was he afraid of the expense or excited at the possibility of achieving his top bucket list goal? Or both? The room was hushed as the tension built. Finally, a guy next to Jed leaned over and said, "Good luck. I hope you get it. I can't bear to see another art masterpiece disappear into a billionaire's treasure trove on the other side of the planet."

"Thanks," he said, offering a weak smile. He turned and looked over his shoulder at his competitor. The man would whisper into his cellphone, then listen, like a quarterback getting his coach's instructions for one last play in the Super Bowl.

Sally Stillman waited patiently for an answer. Finally, the man nodded and said, "I bid $11.5 million."

Jed's heart sank. Then he looked around the room and saw that all eyes were focused on him. The others who had dropped out were smiling, nodding, or offering thumb-ups. One former bidder mouthed 'kill him,' as if it were a blood sport. Jed had become the favorite, and the energy in the room lifted him to the edge of his seat.

"Do I hear $11,600,000?"

The auctioneer looked at Jed, then scanned the room.

"Going once."

Again, Stillman locked her eyes on Jed, waiting for a nod.

"Going twice."

Feeling dizzy, Jed closed his eyes. He desperately wanted to win, but at what cost to himself, Lexi and their lifestyle?

Jed opened his eyes, looked back at his competitor, and lifted the paddle from his lap. The man saw him and bid $12 million.

Reality set in. Jed's dream was dead. Jed shook his head once, then again, then one last time.

"Sold to the gentleman in the back," Stillman said, then tapped the gavel on the podium, signaling the end of the auction. "Congratulations."

The winner locked eyes with Jed and mouthed, "Sorry." Jed offered a half smile. He texted a sad emoji to Lexi, who returned a heart with a kiss. Jed looked at his watch and saw that he barely had enough time to get to Oregon Health and Science University Hospital to scrub for surgery. He would replace a defective heart valve in a 29-year-old mother of three in an hour.

4

With his surgical team gathered around the operating table, Jed began a ritual he performed for all his patients before a heart procedure.

"My heart to your heart," said Jed, his hand hovering over, but not touching, the patient's chest. "The heart and soul are one." He looked into the eyes of other doctors and nurses standing around the table, waiting for their refrain.

"Today, we fix a heart and save a soul," they said in unison. "Today, we are one." And the procedure began.

At the beginning of surgery, Jed knew that at least one of his surgical team members had complained about what she called his 'corny, creepy chant.' The surgical chief felt it was an uplifting exercise and agreed with Jed that it helped elevate the importance of every patient. Jed had noticed the complaining nurse never repeated the phrase with other surgical team members. He let it go.

After surgery, Jed met with the patient's husband and parents. He gave them the good news that surgery was successful, there were no complications, and the patient would recover fully. He predicted she would have a long life. They hugged Jed, then each other, before breaking down in tears of joy. Finally, he smiled and stepped away.

Jed double-timed to his office, where he pulled out his personal laptop and logged into the Dark Web with his Cardinal 14 username and password. The Dark Web, a part of the internet not cataloged by search engines like Google, is used for legal and illegal activities. He knew he could be anonymous. An alert was waiting for him in a rare bird poaching room. "Package will arrive this week. Last payment due before delivery." The message ended with a note that the acquisition had resulted in the death of a bird preservation ranger who tried to stop the transaction.

"No one is supposed to get hurt," Jed wrote. "That's our deal. Your team screwed up. Don't let it happen again, or the money stops flowing." He signed The Cardinal. His response included instructions for reparations to the family.

Finally, he logged out of the Dark Web and into his email account. Bill Masterson, the co-chair of the C-14 Foundation's search for a new avian veterinarian, wrote, "I found a candidate with a sketchy past and lots of relevant experience. His name is Jim Briggs. I set up a meeting for this week."

Jed closed his laptop, picked up his phone, and texted Lexi. "Cherry, I'm on my way home. Prepare to celebrate."

"Can't wait," she responded. "At the firing range. Be home in an hour."

CHAPTER 3

Jansen

1

Portland Police Bureau Detective Kim Jansen walked into Chief Detective Mark Larson's office, closed the door, and flopped into a chair.

"What's wrong?" Larson asked.

"Nothing major, and that's the problem. Instead, I'm getting a steady diet of burglaries, the homeless harassing tourists, vandalism, and missing persons," Jansen said. "We need a good murder."

"Don't say that. It's bad luck. Besides, you're about to leave for two weeks of vacation with your mom skiing and goofing off."

"Yes, and I can't wait to get out of here. In fact, I was just about to head over to Andy's Firing Pen to practice my target shooting. Some people might call Mom elderly at 65, but she's still a demon on cross-country skis and a crack shot with a biathlon rifle. Mom is trying to make up for not going to the Olympics."

"Why didn't she go?"

"She got pregnant with me."

"You were a troublemaker from the get-go, weren't you?"

"My middle name. By the way, Larson, don't forget Jim and I are meeting you and Meg tonight for a B and B." A B and B was code for beer and bullshit. They would drink, unwind, and update their lives, a tradition Larson and Jansen started when they worked together in the patrol division.

"I wish we could go *now*," he said. "Anything to escape this growing mountain of paper on my desk."

Standing side by side, Jansen and Larson could be fraternal twins. He was a Swede. She was Dutch. Because of their Northern European heritage, they shared genetic traits: light hair, light blue eyes, and were over six feet tall. Larson was 6-feet-4 and Jansen 6-feet-1. When they came late to roll call one day, their sergeant dressed them down in front of the other officers and nicknamed them the Wooden Shoe Blues. He apparently didn't understand that the Swedes didn't wear wooden shoes and bristled when Jansen pointed out the fact. So far, none of the other detectives had the nerve to use the moniker—at least not to their faces.

Before their promotions to the detective bureau, they were partnered as patrol officers. In the six years that followed, they survived two shootouts—one with robbery suspects fleeing a jewelry store and the other outside a convenience store with two meth heads. Each had saved the other's life when pinned down in an exchange of gunfire.

Their temperaments couldn't be more different. He was introverted, quiet, and well-liked on the streets because of his low-key style. He operated by the book. Jansen was a hothead, a loner who was fearless in the field and often broke the rules at her own peril. She had been kicked, punched, and stabbed trying to single-handedly subdue suspects. A chipped front tooth, a cracked rib, and a long scar on her abdomen were a testament to her rough-and-tumble style. Small scars on her right leg were from shrapnel when a fellow soldier stepped on a land mine during her Army tour in Afghanistan.

The deep, red scar on her belly resulted from a stab wound she had suffered a year earlier. She had responded to assist another officer who had stopped a robbery suspect believed to be armed. While the other officer kept his gun trained on the suspect, Jansen moved behind him and closed one handcuff on the man's wrist. She ordered him to show the other hand. When his hand came back, he was gripping a hunting knife, which he swung and used to stab her repeatedly in her pregnant belly before the covering officer fired and killed him. She was in intensive care for the next four weeks, clinging to life after nearly bleeding out at the scene. Doctors could not save her baby. The incident review determined that Jansen had failed to follow protocol to search for a weapon. Eight months pregnant, she had difficulty bending over or moving close, so she skipped the standard frisking procedure. She told the review board she thought she had the suspect under control. They suggested she should have been on desk duty because of her pregnancy. She shrugged at the comment rather than argue.

"Jansen, get out of here. Go target practice," said Larson. "See you for beers."

"See you, Larson."

"Wait, Jansen. Not a 'Yes, Sir' or a 'Yes, Chief'?"

She turned around, flipped him off, and opened the door. "Thanks for your guidance, Chief Larson. I really appreciate it." Jansen belted out the words so the other detectives could hear her. Larson smiled.

2

Jansen greeted Andy Keller, owner of Andy's Firing Pen, a popular gun range, with a hug. They had been rookies together in the Portland Police Bureau. After he suffered a back injury in a fall off a ladder while cleaning leaves from a gutter, Andy was moved out of the patrol division and was appointed department training officer, a job he hated. So, when a local private gun range came up for sale, he jumped on it. He won a contract for his facility to act as the police target and practice range.

"You qualified with your service weapon on your last visit," said Andy. "What's going on?" She unzipped a rifle case, slid out an Anschutz 1827, the preferred rifle for professional biathletes, and handed it to him. Andy looked it over and said, "This is a .22-caliber. A peashooter. Are you going rabbit hunting?"

"It's the Ferrari of biathlete weapons," said Jansen.

"I never understood that sport," said Andy.

"Think of it as a race on skis with a target shooting competition along the way. You race full speed, your heart pounding like a hammer, then you stop and shoot from either a prone or standing position. The target for prone shooting is less than two inches wide. You get five shots. The penalty for every miss is additional distance added to your ski run. Yes, it's a peashooter, but an expensive one for $5,000 to get all the bells and whistles."

"You're not a biathlete," said Andy. "You're barely an athlete if I recall your poor workout schedule when working together."

"Hilarious, but I'm flying back to Wisconsin next week to hang out with my mom who is an excellent biathlete. My ski gear and winter clothes are already packed and in the back of my car."

"I hope you have a great time," said Andy.

A loud crack pierced the noise generated by a half dozen other shooters from the other end of the range. Jansen looked down the row and saw a lone red-headed woman shouldering what looked like an elephant gun. The woman's target was at 100 yards, and the bullets consistently hit the middle ring.

"Who's that?" Jansen asked.

"That's Lexi Miller," said Andy. "AKA Cherry, nicknamed after the Cherry-Throated Tanager, an extremely rare bird. Don't ask me how I know. Apparently, it's part of a bedroom ritual. The name fits. How many women do you know who relish big game trophy hunts in Africa? She has bagged rhinos, hippos, and bull elephants. She's also a champion pistol shooter. The rifle she's shooting is a beauty—a John Rigby bolt-action back, sighted up to 250 yards. The stock is Turkish Walnut. She's shooting a nitro load. Cost: $50K."

Jansen whistled. "Holy shit. Impressive price and firepower."

While Jansen watched Lexi shooting, she saw her stop, read something on her cell phone, then quickly pack up the rifle and head for the exit.

As Lexi walked by Jansen, Andy stopped her. "Hey, Lexi, I want you to meet Kim Jansen. Kim is a detective for the Portland Police Bureau."

Lexi reached out and gave Jansen a firm handshake. She squeezed Jansen's hand like a man, attempting to establish dominance with a firm grip. Jansen was accustomed to shaking hands with beefy male cops and knew how to play the game. She squeezed back with just the right amount of force. Lexi, who was nearly as tall as Jansen, smiled in appreciation. Two strong women, forces to be reckoned with.

"Nice to meet you," said Lexi. "My husband just texted me. He says he has a surprise at home. I suspect it's an early birthday present. I'm eager to get home."

"Happy birthday," said Jansen.

"Not sure how you can be happy about turning 50, but thanks."

"Happy day," said Andy.

After Lexi left the range, Andy said, "Her husband, Jed, is a heart surgeon. They're a Portland power couple. They donate a lot to the Portland Audubon Society. The Millers and their friends are all about birding, 24/7. If you ask me, birding is for the birds. Who wants to walk around their backyard or a local park looking for birds? I'd rather tweet. And I hate social media."

"Me, too," said Jansen, smiling at Andy's word play. "Nice catching up with you, Andy, but I better get busy with my target practice, or I'll embarrass myself when I'm shooting with my mom and her friends next week."

3

Jansen unlocked the front door and walked into the living room of her 4,000-square-foot luxury townhouse in Portland's Pearl District. She would be lucky to afford even one of the four bedrooms on her salary. Her husband, Jim Briggs, had inherited the place after his mother died. Fully paid for, Jansen and Briggs had minimal expenses except for the property taxes, which had hit $15,000 annually. With so much tax money, she wondered why the city couldn't afford more staffing for the Portland Police Bureau. She knew some answers: COVID-19, city hall's mixed messages about how the cops should respond to the Black Lives Matter protests, and a lack of action against Antifa's crusade to destroy the city. All of this had soured the public appetite for more police and demoralized officers. Retirements and resignations left the ranks decimated. Jansen guessed that restoring the once vibrant Portland and its police force could take decades.

Inside the front door, Jansen listened for Briggs. Rather than yell—their home was so cavernous that Briggs couldn't hear her when he was in his office at the back of the house—she used their intercom to find him. "In the kitchen," he said.

Jansen walked into the kitchen and over to Briggs. She reached up, grabbed him by his red beard with both hands, and gently pulled him toward her for a kiss. He didn't resist. Although Jansen was over six feet, Briggs towered over her at 6-feet-6.

"What's that for?" said Briggs.

"I love you," said Jansen.

"I love you, too, Jansen.

"Are you sick or having a breakdown of some kind?"

"What do you mean?" Jansen asked, looking serious.

"I can't remember when you've been this relaxed and cuddly," said Briggs.

"Maybe my impending vacation has softened me."

"I like it," said Briggs.

"Don't get used to it," said Jansen, who worked hard to disguise her vulnerabilities, even with Briggs.

He wrapped his arms around her. "Get ready for dinner. We have a chicken curry stir fry with brown rice, a side of asparagus, a dry Riesling, and gingerbread with whipped cream for dessert."

"You might get some extra dessert at bedtime for a dinner like that," said Jansen, raising her eyebrows. "I have to clean up. Ten minutes in the shower, and I'll be down for that glass of wine."

After locking up her gun, showering, and changing into sweats, Jansen returned to the kitchen. Briggs had set the table, poured the wine, and had plated the dinner when he saw her walk into the room.

"Here's to escaping the grind," said Jansen. They lifted their glasses and ate in silence for a few minutes.

"I've already told you nothing much was happening in my world," said Jansen. "What about you?"

Two years before, Briggs had launched *Have Paws—Will Travel*, a mobile dog care service. Wealthy clients paid him a monthly retainer plus expenses for 24-hour concierge care. In response to a request in his mother's will, Briggs also helped the dogs of Portland's homeless for free. Eventually, overwhelmed by the needs of the homeless, Briggs cut back his charitable program from three days to one day a week and switched his focus to avian medicine. He used his extra time to recruit new clients who wanted him to care for their birds. He thought his avian medicine training at Oregon State University's Carlton School of Veterinary Medicine would improve the quality of his life.

"I've struck gold," said Briggs.

Jansen cocked her head and waited for more.

"The C-14 Foundation, a bird preservation group, called me for an interview to replace their recently deceased bird vet. The Foundation is offering a six-figure annual salary, with a $50,000 signing bonus, to care for the birds of its members. It's part-time."

"Wow," said Jansen. "Golden handcuffs. What does C-14 stand for?"

"I did a web search and found out that Jed Miller, Foundation co-founder, said he saw his first Northern Cardinal when he was 14 while visiting his great aunt down south. And get this. The Foundation has 14 members, half men, and half women. Mostly couples. All rich. They call themselves the Red Flock. They love rare birds with red coloring."

"That's bizarre. They're putting you on."

"I'll find out. I meet tomorrow with Miller and Bill Masterson, co-chair of the committee handling the search for a new vet."

"Is Jed Miller a heart surgeon?"

"Yep. That's the guy. Why?"

"I met his wife, Lexi Miller, at Andy's today when I went there for target practice. Andy said the Millers and their friends are loaded. They donate a ton of cash for birding causes."

"And potentially a boatload of cash for us," said Briggs. He told her about the non-disclosure agreement he had signed before they would schedule an interview.

"They're swearing me to secrecy. I can't discuss the job or what's said during the interview to anyone, including you."

"They sound like the CIA. Why would a benevolent foundation set up to protect birds around the world have secrets?"

"My guess is money," said Briggs. "Rich people can be very protective of their financial information. Most of my dog care clients are that way. Send them a bill, and they pay, no questions asked but they don't want to talk about money."

"Just be careful and back away from the deal if you think it's hinky."

"How about that extra dessert you mentioned earlier?" Briggs asked. "Did you want to handcuff me, Detective, or do I get to use my hands?"

"I'm too exhausted for bedroom games. Show me the way. And show me what you've got. I won't resist."

"Hmmm. I think I have something in mind that will help you sleep tonight."

Jansen smiled, took Briggs' hand, and followed him into the bedroom.

CHAPTER 4

Lexi

1

Lexi went to her walk-in closet and pulled out a drawer to get her costume for the celebration. Jed hadn't told her what the celebration was for—her birthday or something else—but they would discuss that after they completed their ritual. When he called her "Cherry," it meant passionate sex.

Before dressing in her bird costume, she stood naked in front of a mirror, assessing her body. Not bad for a woman turning 50. Breasts are not as perky. Ass a little less firm and a bit of belly fat. But overall, damn good. Jed said her body was super fine. She felt the same about his body. Jed was naturally lean, still a stud, but he also had a little extra fat here and there, despite a rigorous workout routine. Content with her body assessment, she began suiting up for their celebration.

Lexi pushed her legs into a cherry red, skin-tight jumpsuit and zipped it to her chin. She added a matching hood, tucking in her dark red hair, so only a bit of her face was visible. Finally she added a mask with feathers she had painted to look like a Cherry-Throated Tanager. "I'm ready," she texted Jed.

"On my way," Jed texted. Their sprawling, 5,000-square-foot home in Portland's West Hills had all the latest communications gadgets, at Jed's insistence, including intelligent assistants in every room to answer their questions, create reminders, and play music. When Jed asked Lexi a question, Alexa frequently interrupted with an answer. It was maddening.

Texts were less invasive, they agreed, especially when Lexi was painting. During creative bursts, she kept her phone in the do-not-disturb mode or allowed it to vibrate for important notifications.

In anticipation of Jed's arrival, she walked to the end of the bed and stood at attention.

Jed knocked and walked into Lexi's bedroom. He was wearing an identical red suit. His mask was painted to look like a male Northern Cardinal. In his hand was the Daisy Red Ryder BB gun he got on his 14th birthday. It was nicked and dented from endless use during his two summers in Tennessee.

Killing the cardinal had flipped a switch in Jed's psyche, evident the first time they made love. They had met in college at a costume party fundraiser for the local Audubon Society Chapter. Guests wore bird masks. His was a cardinal, hers an American Red Flamingo. When the fundraiser ended, they spent the night having sex in her dorm room with masks on.

Jed lifted the BB gun, shouldered it, and aimed it at Lexi. She stood still, turning her head to look out of one eye like a bird. "My heart to your heart," he said. "Our hearts are one." Then, there was a popping sound. Lexi spun around, held out her arms like they were wings—recreating the scene from Jed's youth— and fell on the floor. Jed lifted her onto the bed, and they began undressing each other. The masks stayed on. When they finished, they laid back and looked up at the ceiling.

"That was great, Babe," said Lexi. "But don't you think this dress-up routine is getting stale? Shouldn't we save it for our anniversary—once a year?"

"It still turns me on," he said. "Let's think about it. Meanwhile, you're probably wondering what we're celebrating."

"My birthday."

"No. But don't worry. I haven't forgotten it."

She looked at him, waiting for the reveal.

"Bill Masterson's Orange-Bellied Parrot arrived at the port of entry and has been cleared. Delivery is scheduled for this week. I've already transferred the final payment to the acquisition team."

"Great news. We're approaching our goal to fill all C-14 member rare bird requests."

"Not so great news is that a bird preservation ranger was killed attempting to stop the capture," said Jed. "I fired an email back to our contact and blistered his ass. I told him that couldn't happen again. And I told him he needed to pay the ranger's family for their loss. So, I'm giving them $10,000. For an indigenous person living in Tasmania, where Orange-Bellied Parrots are born, $10,000 could be equal to 10 years of income."

"Helping the victim's family is the least we can do," Lexi said. "We've been importing rare birds to fill Red Flock requests for nearly two years. We tell people the Foundation is about bird preservation when it's really about a pack of selfish millionaires who want to own rare birds. We know it's illegal as hell and police will hunt us down if we aren't careful. We're in big legal trouble if we're ever caught."

"I wouldn't worry about that too much," said Jed. "We'll tighten security and replace some workers. They're getting careless. I'm glad we haven't had more loss of life."

"In the meantime, I'll work on our upcoming gathering of the Red Flock," said Lexi.

"More important, we need to talk about the auction and *The Birds of America*," said Jed. "We got so close."

"We might be close to another one," said Lexi. "I'll tell you more later. Let's shower and meet back here for lunch."

"How's that possible?" asked Jed.

"Over lunch," she said. "Go shower."

2

Their chef served a lunch of spinach salad with tarragon chicken slices, fresh fruit, and passion fruit iced tea.

Jed looked at her and said, "I'm sorry about the auction. There was just no way we could afford $12 million. Ten million would be stretching it. Another Audubon will eventually come up for sale."

Lexi reached over and put her hand on his. "It's okay, babe. It just so happens another book has come up for sale, just in time for your birthday." The Millers were Capricorns, their January birthdays a week apart.

Jed's mouth dropped open, then closed. She was kidding him. A cruel joke, he thought.

"My dear Cherry baby, where on Earth would we get another copy of *Birds of America*? We know that only 10 of the existing 120 copies are in private hands. The rest are in libraries and art museums. As far as I know, no more private copies have come up for sale."

Lexi filled him in on the deal. "Bruce McQuillan, the owner of McQuillan's Books downtown, called and left a message saying he knew of a set in private hands and the book's owner was ready to make a sale. He said his brother, Dan, would step in for him to finalize the arrangements. I immediately called Dan, who said Bruce had been recovering from a heart attack and was not doing well. But he confirmed we're moving forward."

"How much?"

"Two million."

"You mean $12 million?"

"No, it's two."

He started to probe but stopped. Instead, he smiled and said, "You're amazing. Shall we go back to bed for another celebration?"

"On one condition: no costume and no mask. We can have a celebration if and when the deal goes through."

Jed grabbed her hand and headed down the hall. They looked at each other and raced to the bedroom like two hormone-engorged teens.

3

For Jed, possessing *The Birds of America* would be a status symbol. For Lexi, it would be an opportunity to establish herself as one of the world's great wildlife painters. It was an outrageous goal given her lack of commercial success. When her friend Angela Simmons, owner of the Simmons Art Gallery, offered Lexi a showing of her red bird paintings, Lexi's spent months preparing an exhibition she called, *The Red Flock*.

Reviews were tepid. A single painting sold at half price. On closing night, when everyone had left, Lexi slid down the wall onto the floor and burst into tears. Simmons raced over to console her. After Lexi had stopped crying,

Simmons explained the event hadn't failed for lack of talent. Instead, she praised Lexi for having more talent than many who had sold their art in her gallery for ungodly amounts. Lexi needed to build a reputation and a following, Simmons said.

"Invest time and money in marketing yourself and your talent. Find influencers who will praise your work. People want to impress their friends. They want their peers to view them as astute investors who recognize good art when they see it. It's not enough to be great. Others must acknowledge your greatness."

Lexi agreed with Simmons that publicity was important, but she was still convinced her path to greatness linked to John James Audubon's work.

4

Lexi had known for some time what she had to do: get a copy of *The Birds of America*, create an updated version of the book, and win worldwide praise for her work. The art world would hail her paintings as ground-breaking, displayed side-by-side with Audubon's paintings in art exhibitions.

At least that was her dream. The past week, she had tried to copy one of Audubon's most straightforward bird paintings from a reprint and failed. She blamed it on the poor quality of the print. She decided she needed the real thing to emulate if she was going to accomplish her goals. Lexi's painting, she admitted, lacked the sensuality of Audubon's. His birds jumped off the page, larger than life. Hers were flat. She crumpled up her work and threw it in the corner of her studio.

"I need the real paintings to study and learn how to capture the light that brings the birds to life," she said to her Frenchie, Trudy. "You agree, don't you, girl?" Trudy didn't run over and jump in her lap like she usually would. She was droopy. Lexi picked her up and set her on her lap. "You okay, girl?" Trudy's head lifted, then dropped back to Lexi's lap. Lexi was about to phone Ian Reid to come check out Trudy, then remembered he had died. She dearly missed him. Now, she'd have to find someone new.

While petting Trudy, her mind jumped back to the first time she saw an original of *The Birds of America*. It was in the John Wilson Collections, the rare book room at the Portland Central Library. She had made an appointment with Marc Stanfield, who allowed her to come in, page through the books, make sketches and take photographs. One visit wasn't enough. She went back more than a dozen times, often bringing her own paintings to hold next to Audubon's originals. Hers lacked vibrance. The difference frustrated her.

She eventually shared her dream of owning a copy with Stanfield. He confided that if he could afford to buy an original Audubon, his marital and financial problems would disappear. Lexi remembered them looking at each other and nodding as if they had just figured out the answer to their prayers.

CHAPTER 5

Bruce

1

In a week, Bruce McQuillan would be dead. His brother, Dan, would help him die. Bruce's daughter, Meg, would mourn the loss. All of them would benefit, especially Meg, Bruce decided.

Bruce struggled to his feet, his COPD from a lifelong smoking habit and lung cancer sapping his energy, squeezing the life out of him. An oxygen bottle affixed to his walker was life's last thin thread. The heart attack he had suffered a year earlier assured his early exit. Finally, at 66, he was at death's door. But, before he opened that door, he needed to wrap up a few loose ends, giving Dan and Meg the inheritance they deserved.

Dan had never been interested in working in the bookstore their grandfather had founded at the end of the Great Depression. Granddad McQuillan's plan was to provide a living for himself and all future generations. Each generation would take over from the last. The plan worked great for two generations and looked promising for a third when Bruce joined his dad in the business. But the plan fell apart when Dan joined the Army.

After a six-year tour of duty that turned him into one of the military's most fearsome snipers—with no home and no place to go—Dan returned to Portland. Bruce welcomed Dan's help in the bookstore, but their father was skeptical it would last. Dad was right. Dan's career as a bookman lasted precisely one week. Mostly, he fought with his dad, who still hadn't forgiven him for joining the Army. Dan confided to Bruce that he found the bookstore claustrophobic and depressing. Shortly after quitting, he launched a two-year trek. Dan traveled through the Alps, then into Nepal's high passes. He completed the 500-mile France to Spain Camino de Santiago walk before settling back in the U.S. On that trip, he met and married a Spanish-speaking elementary school teacher traveling alone on holiday in Spain. A year later, he divorced her and returned to school to improve his accounting skills. He had an accounting degree but had not used it for over a decade. Although he was a numbers whiz— the talent their Dad and Bruce needed to manage a million-book inventory— Dan confided to Bruce that he would never return to McQuillan's. Instead, he worked for a few years at one big company or another as an accounting temp, saved his money, then launched into one new adventure after another.

"Sit down, Dan," said Bruce. "Let's have a wee dram of scotch."

Bruce held up the bottle to show him the label: Macallan, 30-year aged, $6,000 a bottle.

"I took it in trade for a first edition of Charles Dickens's *The Christmas Story* that happened across my desk."

"Happened across your desk?" Dan said, arching his eyebrows.

Bruce winked, took a sip, and let the peaty flavor settle on his tongue. Dan swirled the glass in the overhead light and gulped it like a man drowning in a swimming pool. He was there to assist his brother's suicide. He needed to numb himself before Bruce swallowed the fatal dose of barbiturate. Bruce had acquired the drugs legally under Oregon's Death with Dignity Act. Everything was in order. Still, helping your brother kill himself was unlike killing a terrorist from a thousand yards with a sniper rifle. This was up close and personal.

Bruce poured each of them two fingers more. Dan didn't object.

"Danny, thanks for sticking around long enough to finish *The Birds of America* deal. There's no one I would trust more to protect Meghan's future. And, of course, you'll be set for life."

"Listen up, big brother. I'll be here for Meg. Whatever she needs. But after working with her for the past few weeks, I know she won't need handholding. You've raised a strong, independent woman. I reviewed your accounts, as you asked, and you'll be happy to know that some of her new marketing strategies are working. Using her library connections, she found a student willing to manage online sales of rare books and magazines in exchange for experience. Meg also is scheduling book club meetings and speakers to attract buyers willing to pay full price for a new hardback edition. As a result, sales are up 20 percent. Still, she has a long way to go before she can call this a going concern."

"I feel better about leaving, knowing that Meg might pull off a turnaround."

2

Bruce and Dan had always been close, even though they had seen little of one another over the previous three decades. When they saw each other, they loved to recall the old days when they were wild kids playing hide-and-seek in McQuillan's endless book stacks. Mostly they were hiding from their dad, who treated them like his full-time workers, while paying less than the minimum wage.

When Bruce willed half the store to Dan, he hoped Dan might jump in as co-manager with Meg, using his financial prowess to prevent bankruptcy.

"Dan, my will leaves the store to you and Meg, a 50-50 split. After all, Dad unfairly cut you out of the business for no other reason than it didn't fit his plan. I inherited everything, mainly the books in this store and many faithful customers. But online stores and the COVID-19 pandemic stopped the flow of customers for more than a year. The money in used books and magazines isn't paying the rent."

"Are you suggesting I settle down and help run the bookstore into the ground?"

Bruce took Dan's hand. "You two can shut it down, sell off the books, and you can move on to new adventures. Granddad McQuillan's investment 80 years ago already has paid off in job security. You have to admit that got the family through The Great Depression and created a nice base of support when Dad married and had us."

"Any chance Meg could return to her old library job?" Dan asked.

"I don't think they'll take her back after she resigned just days after a promotion. She abandoned her career to take my place while I recovered. That killed her career. It was selfish on my part. I should have shut it down and hired someone to liquidate the inventory."

"Bruce, don't be so hard on yourself. You're wasting energy on what-ifs. Are you sure you want to go through with this? Once you take the pills, there's no turning back."

"Think about it, brother. I'm nearly dead. A massive heart attack is likely to take me any day. If the cops found out I was involved in the theft of the Audubon books, I'd spend my last few days in a courtroom or in jail. So, I want to pick the time and place of my death.

I wrote Meg a letter and gave it to my attorney. She'll get it during the will reading. I've paid for cremation. You and Meg can dump my ashes any place you like. Just not downstairs in the basement." They both laughed.

Bruce opened a vial and looked at the pills his doctor had prescribed. A smile crossed his face. He poured them into his hand. "Here's to you, Danny," he said as he swallowed them with a scotch chaser.

"Danny, you'd think the grim reaper would be scary, wouldn't you?"

"I can't imagine."

"Because you're healthy. You can see a future. My world has been closing in on me, especially as my lungs fail. All of this and the cancer are creating so much damn pain. These pills are going to save your old brother. Allow me to ease out of this miserable life."

"Any regrets?"

"Wish I had shared some adventures with you. The Spain trek must have been heaven. But you probably wouldn't have met your Sadie and gotten married if I had gone."

"Meeting Sadie was heaven, then hell. I wish you had come. Would have saved me some pain."

"Who knows where death will take me? Maybe I'll be in a permanent dream state, taking endless adventures like you have. Then, I'll be ready for whatever comes." His tongue was getting thick.

Dan held his hand. "I love you, Bruce."

"I love you, too."

"One more thing," said Bruce. "Come closer."

Bruce was beginning to fade. Dan couldn't help thinking a deathbed confession was coming. And that's exactly what happened. He put his ear to Bruce's mouth and listened to his final words. What he heard made Dan's head jerked back as if he had seen the devil. He looked at his brother's face. Bruce forced his eyes open and nodded that what he told him was true. Bruce smiled and, a moment later, was unconscious. Dan said in a low voice, "It's okay. I'll take care of everything."

Bruce hung on for 30 minutes before the drug stopped his heart, so the process was quick and painless.

Dan felt for a pulse. When he found none, he said, "I won't let you down, big brother. Godspeed. See you in the next life."

Dan straightened the bed, neatened the room, then called the coroner's office and the funeral home. Bruce had left detailed instructions. In his brother's planning for death, Dan recognized one of Bruce's superpowers: his clear-eyed view of the world and his ability to see details others missed.

While he waited for the hearse and the coroner, he phoned Meg to give her the news. Then he texted Lexi Miller about completing the sale of *The Birds of America*. "We need to talk. There's a price change. $5 million."

CHAPTER 6

Lexi

1

The text from Dan Miller was a punch in the chest. Lexi had a deal with Bruce McQuillan, she thought, for $2 million. Now, his brother wanted more. No doubt he saw the local news about the auction of *The Birds of America* for $12 million.

"Dammit," she yelled. Her dog, Trudy, jumped up, ears perked. "I want those bird books, and I want them for the price quoted. A deal is a deal."

She texted an anger emoji to Dan and threw her phone across the room. The phone landed with a loud crack on the tile floor. Lexi groaned. She knew she had cracked the screen, the third this year in fits of pique. She looked at Trudy, who was cowering. "Sorry, girl, I know you're not feeling well. It's okay." Trudy laid down.

Despite Dan McQuillan's attempt to extort her, Lexi distracted herself with the details of the next gathering of the Red Flock. She sent a group email confirming the time and date, the menu, and a photo of the critically endangered Orange-Bellied Parrot that Bill Masterson would receive at the meeting. All of the members were good personal friends who loved birds with red feathers. Most had favorite red birds but weren't fixated like Jed. Instead, they humored his obsession with the Northern Red Cardinal. The Flock also indulged Lexi's painting passion and desire to own a Cherry-Throated Tanager, both of which were the result of an eclectic childhood.

Lexi's parents were linguists and professors who thought it would be cute to name their only child Lexicon. They spent their sabbaticals studying and recording languages in Central and South America for scientific papers, lectures, and books they would co-author. Lexi went everywhere with them.

When she was ten, her parents took her to Brazil. A side trip into the Atlantic Rainforest left Lexi thunderstruck. There among the region's 1,000 bird species was one that she could never forget. From high in the tree canopy came a sharp call that caught her attention. Then she saw it. A bird with striking plumage: white crown, black band wrapping its head with a bright red patch on its neck and flowing down its chest, like blood from a neck wound. Their Portuguese-speaking guide called it a saira-apunhalada or "stabbed tanager" because of its vivid red throat. He said the bird, officially dubbed the Cherry-Throated Tanager, was discovered in 1870 and not seen again until 1941. The American Bird Conservancy estimated only 30 birds existed, declaring them critically endangered. Lexi knew even as a kid that she had to have one for her growing aviary back home. Her parents said they were rare and wild and should stay in the forest.

When Jed heard about Lexi's Tanager sighting as a kid, he began calling her Cherry. At first, she thought the nickname was cute—until a close friend told Lexi that Cherry sounded like a porn star or stripper. So she told Jed he could only use it during their celebrations in the bedroom.

After years of leading exotic birding trips for their best friends, Lexi suggested forming a foundation to protect endangered bird species. So Jed and their friend Bill Masterson developed C-14, the Cardinal 14 Foundation. They agreed membership would be limited to 14: Jed, Lexi, Masterson and his wife, and ten of their closest friends and birding companions. Between Jed's contacts and Masterson's prominence in birding circles, recruiting the members was easy. Masterson was the owner/founder of a massive online birding supply company. He sold everything from field guides and clothes to footwear and spotting scopes for backyard birders as well as those, like the Millers, who traveled worldwide to see rare birds. Masterson's company was so profitable that a large animal products firm offered him $1.2 billion to buy his business. He thanked the company executives and said he would circle back in a few years when he was ready to retire.

Under C-14 Foundation bylaws, each member paid $1 million a year. Initially, Foundation projects focused on bird habitat restoration and wildlife protection. Five million dollars went annually to the National Audubon Society, with other significant contributions to the Land Trust, World Wildlife Foundation, Greenpeace, the Climate Foundation, and Rainforest Action Network. Then Lexi suggested expanding the concept. After some debate, she convinced the members that acquiring endangered birds would help save the species. Within months, members had submitted their requests for rare birds, and Jed plugged into a poaching network.

Each acquisition varied from $100,000 to $500,000, depending on the rarity of the bird species. The Orange-Bellied Parrot that Masterson ordered from Tasmania was $500,000. When a bird was delivered, the Red Flock held a ritual wearing red bird costumes, followed by an elaborate dinner. The menus were always bird related, from foie gras appetizers to ostrich egg soup.

2

With the invitations out to the Red Flock to celebrate the arrival of Bill Masterson's parrot, Lexi set her sights on concluding the sale of the Audubon books.

After the last copy of the books went for a record sum, Lexi knew $2 million was a pittance—a great deal. Twice that much would be a steal. When Bruce McQuillan approached her, he seemed like a straight shooter. Without haggling, he set a price, requested a 10 percent down payment, and stayed in touch. Periodically, McQuillan sent an email to her that the sale date was getting closer. Then Bruce threw a monkey wrench into the works: he committed suicide and his greedy brother, Dan, stepped in to complete the deal.

Who the hell was this guy? she wondered.

"I think this Dan is a dirty dealer," she told Jed, who looked up from the travel brochure he was studying to find future Red Flock birding trips. "He can't be trusted."

"Babe, give it your best shot," he said.

She pulled out her phone and texted Dan McQuillan, "Let's complete the deal. Meet me tomorrow at Andy's Firing Pen at 2 pm. You can't miss me. Red hair and a big gun. The deal is $2 million, not a penny more."

"I won't see you tomorrow or ever until you accept the new price," Dan responded. "I've got no hair and a big gun." The standoff was set.

Lexi had hoped the thinly-veiled threat would back Dan away from his inflated price. Instead, he came right back at her. What if he figured he could push the deal a few million higher? Should she go along with it?

No! Never. A plan of attack flooded her mind. This required a big statement of just how serious she was about keeping the original deal's terms.

Trudy jumped up in her lap. "We're going to give Dan hell, aren't we?" she said, lifting the dog to her face. Trudy licked her.

"Thanks, girl. Glad you agree."

"How about Bwindi Impenetrable Forest in Uganda?" Jed asked.

Lexi looked up and cocked her head. "What are you talking about?"

"The next adventure for the Flock. Uganda or the Bangweulu Swamps in Zambia?"

"Swamps sound dreadful," said Lexi.

"You're getting soft, my little tanager."

"And so are our friends, the older they get."

"Doñana National Park in Spain," he said. "They have a red-knobbed coot that looks interesting."

"The food alone is a reason to go there," said Lexi. "We can discuss it with the Flock at our next gathering."

CHAPTER 7

Jim

Jim Briggs drove his *Have Paws—Will Travel* mobile canine care van up the long, steep road to the Miller's Portland West Hills estate and stopped in front of a massive metal gate with a two-foot-high letter M. As instructed, Jim phoned Jed to announce his arrival. A moment later, the gate swung inward, allowing him to pass. He drove up to a circular driveway and parked. He stepped out just as the front door swung open, and Miller came out to greet him.

Miller extended his hand and said, "Welcome, Jim."

"Thanks," said Jim, his giant paw meeting Jed's firm grip.

Although Jed was over six feet with broad shoulders and a body molded by triathlons and marathon bike rides, Jim towered over him.

"Follow me," said Jed. "My colleague, Bill Masterson, will join us today for our interview."

The Miller home was open and airy. The entryway widened into a long hallway covered with murals of lush, tropical forest scenes. Light poured in from skylights and large windows, each with a view of the city below and Forest Park, Portland's 5,000-acre urban forest. The home's orientation emphasized its integration with the surrounding forest.

Toward the end of the hallway, Jed stopped at a glass wall. Inside was a tropical paradise of lush greenery and exotic birds. Most of the birds were tropical. All had splashes of red, including 14 Northern Cardinals.

"Interesting mix of birds," said Jim.

"Guess you're wondering how the cardinals fit," said Jed. "They're my favorite since I was a kid. I love the color." He didn't offer more.

Jed led Jim into his office, a 1000-square-foot room with minimalist furnishings. Unlike the rich colors throughout the house, the room was white with a glass meeting table.

Jed introduced Masterson, who shook hands with Jim and asked him to sit down. Individual cheese and fruit plates, and a Byrne Vineyards 2016 Pinot Noir bottle were on the table.

"My wife Kim and I love Byrne wines."

"Are you attending the Byrne Free-as-a Bird party tomorrow?" asked Jed.

"We'll be there." He didn't explain that Kim had arrested Colin Byrne the year before for conspiracy to steal rare books as part of a family vendetta. Byrne argued he had been a victim of intergenerational violence. Still, the jury found him guilty. The judge sentenced him to one year in jail, despite the prosecutor's call for five years. The wine party was a celebration of Byrne's return as CEO, following his early release.

They each took a sip of wine.

"Bill will explain the C-14 Foundation and why we need a veterinarian with avian medicine experience."

For the next few minutes, Bill talked about the Foundation's mission to provide and restore bird habitat and rescue endangered birds that could no longer survive in the wild.

"Over the past five years, the Foundation's assets have grown to nearly $50 million, and that's after donating $25 million toward preservation," said Bill.

"Impressive," said Jim.

"No doubt you're wondering why the non-disclosure agreement?" asked Jed. "Two reasons: our members want to remain anonymous, and many have private aviaries with endangered birds."

Jim sat up, a red flag flapping in his mind like a matador's cape. He knew that the U.S. Endangered Species Act and corresponding international laws were clear about preventing rare birds' removal from their natural habitat and exporting or importing them.

"How is it possible to obtain endangered birds with all the layers of international oversight?" Jim asked.

Jed glanced at Bill. They had expected the question. The answer, Jim knew, would stay in the room per the non-disclosure.

"The people who manage many of the reserves where the birds are found are desperately short of cash. They need money to pay locals to help restore lost habitats and hire and equip rangers to prevent poaching. That's where we come in. Rather than allow the animals to die, we plug into a network to move them in exchange for contributions."

Jim pushed back. "Authorities aren't likely to see your contributions as philanthropic."

Masterson doubled-down. "Frankly, the government officials in charge of the preservation programs are neither well trained nor have the resources—or the will—to save many of the endangered birds. Our work will do more to protect the threatened species than they can." Jim sat back. He'd let it go—for the moment. Bill and Jed appeared to relax, the question of legality behind them.

"How would I fit into the Foundation's plans?"

"You would keep the imported birds alive and manage the health of the birds in our Foundation member's aviaries," said Jed. "Each of us wants to keep them healthy and prolong their lives as long as possible."

"The job pays $150,000 a year," said Bill. "You can keep your canine practice as long as it doesn't interfere with member bird care. We would expect you to make routine house calls to oversee the health of our birds and be available around the clock for emergencies."

"No doubt you've done your research, so you know that last year my colleague, Helen Williams, committed suicide when police moved in to arrest her for killing a group of homeless men who had raped her. My practice was ground zero for adverse publicity. My license to operate my pet crematory was suspended.

"I was never accused or arrested for what Helen did. She operated without my knowledge. Still, half my clients quit my canine care program. Only one woman explained why she was terminating the service. The other's ghosted me. They stopped the monthly retainer payments and no longer called for care.

"With fewer canine care clients, I added bird care to my services. I chose avian medicine because I gained extensive experience in vet school, diagnosing and caring for birds, especially exotic ones. And I've reduced my charity work for the homeless to make room for my bird practice."

Masterson and Jed looked at each other, then back at Jim, and nodded. They already knew about Jim's problems and appreciated his candor.

"Jim, would you mind stepping out for a minute to allow us to discuss your application?"

Jim got up and walked out to the hallway just in time to see a tall woman with dark red hair coming his way.

"You must be Dr. Briggs. Jed said you were coming to discuss the Foundation's bird care needs. I'm Lexi Miller, Jed's wife and one of the Foundation's founding members. Did he tell you we call ourselves the Red Flock because of our love of birds with red plumage?"

"I like the name," said Jim. He lied. The name was corny, contrived. Something you might expect from eccentric millionaires.

"Look at us," said Jim, standing in front of a large decorative mirror in the hallway.

Lexi looked. "Of course," she laughed. "We're redheads. Do you think Jed is taking this redhead thing too far?" Jim smiled. An intriguing thought. The man was seeing red everywhere.

"Jim, I know you have a practice caring for dogs. Can you look at Trudy? She's panting, sluggish, and not eating, like her stomach is upset. She's in my studio."

He followed Lexi into a gallery of bird paintings and then to an attached studio. An easel held a picture in progress. Trudy looked up. When she saw Briggs, she pulled herself into a sitting position. Then, she offered a low growl, a gentle warning to the giant person approaching.

"Let me take a look," he said, kneeling to pet Trudy. Trudy relaxed after Jim talked to her in a quiet voice. She didn't resist his exam.

"She's dehydrated. Has she been throwing up?"

"I don't know. I haven't seen any evidence of it. But in this big house, she could do it anywhere, and it would be dried before the next visit of our housecleaning crew.

Briggs looked down at his hand and saw a yellow substance. "Looks like paint," he said.

"Oh no! She's been eating paint again. When I'm in my studio working, I have my paints everywhere. No doubt some on the floor where she could reach them."

"That's probably the answer. You need to keep the paint out of reach."

Briggs recommended a soft food diet and lots of water to clean her out. He predicted she would be recovered in a few days.

"I can come back later this week and check on her if you like."

"That would be great."

After a few minutes, Bill Masterson called Briggs back into the office.

"We think you'd be a perfect match for the Foundation as our new veterinarian."

"Our members have authorized a $50,000 signing bonus to the right candidate," said Jed. "We think you're the right candidate."

Jim smiled. "Let me talk it over with my wife, and I'll give you an answer tomorrow."

They shook hands, and Jed led Jim back to his van.

As Jim drove down the driveway, he thought about the pros and cons of the job. The money would be great. About the same as he had earned from a full client list for dog care before they quit, but with a lot less work. He feared legal and ethical problems over the Endangered Species Act. He tried to push away his concern. Still, the pros and cons ping-ponged in his head. His focus would be on bird care, not law enforcement. The Foundation's goal to save birds was admirable. Would an international court see it that way? The job as the C-14's vet would be a sweet deal. But did he want to encourage them to keep rare, endangered bird species?

CHAPTER 8

Jansen

1

Kim Jansen picked up her phone and texted Jim, "Don't forget our B and B with Mark and Meg. I'm heading over there now."

Briggs answered with a thumbs up and "on my way."

Thirty minutes later, the four sat at 10 Barrel Brewing in Portland's Pearl District at a high-top table on the roof.

"Here's to us," said Jansen. "Been too long since we've been out for beers." Everyone raised their glasses and took long drinks. Then they were quiet as they tucked into a pizza dubbed the Viking: tomato sauce, mozzarella, pepperoni, Italian sausage, beer-braised pork, black olives, and pepperoncini.

"Hey Larson, that beer you're drinking looks nasty," Jansen said.

"A Jamaican Me Pumpkin."

Jansen shook her head. Larson loved to try new beers, no matter how crazy they were. The annual holiday ale festival downtown in December offered a candy cane porter, Larson's favorite.

Two years before, Larson, Jansen and Briggs were sitting at the same table with Helen Williams, Larson's new love interest. Helen had agreed to manage Briggs' pet crematory while assisting him with his canine care practice, including helping the homeless.

Briggs didn't know when he hired Helen that a group of homeless men had raped her in a park near her apartment just weeks before. The assault occurred a month after her husband was killed in a freak accident. When homeless men began disappearing, Larson was assigned the case. At first, it appeared the missing were just that: they had left town, moved, or melted into the hundreds of homeless encampments in parks, under bridges, and along city streets. But, when evidence pointed to Helen as a suspect in the death of six homeless people, she committed suicide using dog euthanasia drugs. Larson, Briggs, and Jansen arrived on the scene too late to stop her. As a result, Larson, who thought he had found true love and a life partner, was a mental wreck. His friends felt he might never date again, let alone fall in love.

Enter Meg McQuillan. Larson met her during an investigation and eventually asked her out. They had been together for nearly a year. Meg knew about Helen and the significance of the foursome gathering at the same table. However, she didn't seem to mind. Her long friendship with Jansen helped eliminate tensions among her friends.

"So, what's new with you guys?" asked Meg, her head swiveling toward Briggs and Jansen.

"I'm going on vacation to visit my mom," said Jansen.

"A foundation to protect endangered bird species offered me a job today as their vet," said Briggs. "Pays big bucks and a signing bonus for part-time work."

"Briggs, you didn't tell me you got the job offer," said Jansen, reaching out and punching him on the shoulder.

"I came directly from the interview to meet you guys," said Briggs. "It sounds like a sweet deal. I'll sleep on it and give them my answer tomorrow."

"You're next, Larson," said Jansen. "No one wants to hear about your mounds of paperwork that came with that promotion to chief of detectives. So, tell us something new."

"You won't believe what I'm about to say," said Larson. No one moved.

"I'm in love with Meg," said Larson. Heads—including Meg's—snapped to attention, all eyes on him, waiting for his next words. He turned, got off the stool, down on a knee, and said, "Meghan Anne McQuillan, will you be my wife?"

Meg, who figured long ago she would end up a spinster as a public librarian or selling bags of used books alone at McQuillan's, was speechless. She looked at him, searching his face for deception. Although he was right in front of her, she thought he was talking to someone else.

"Are you sure?" she stuttered.

"Should I ask again?"

"No." She looked around. The pub had gotten quiet, everyone waiting for her answer.

"Yes. Yes. Yes. I would love to marry you."

A cheer filled the rooftop terrace. Megan blushed as Larson stood up, hugged her, and kissed her.

"No ring?" asked Jansen.

"Almost forgot," Larson said, red-faced.

He pulled out a platinum ring with an emerald setting, Meg's birthstone, and placed it on her finger.

"I love it," she said. "It's beautiful. And I love you, too."

Just then, Meg's phone rang. She looked at the screen and picked it up.

"It's Uncle Dan. He's helping me run the business, filling in for Dad."

Meg walked over to a quieter area and answered the call.

"Uncle Dan, what's up?" An edge in her voice told him she was annoyed at the interruption.

"Bruce is dead," said Dan, with no soft lead-up, like the cliched 'sorry to be the bearer of bad news.'

"Oh my god. It can't be. I saw Dad last night."

"The coroner is on her way," he said. "I'll tell you everything when you get here."

"Did he fall?" she asked.

"Meg, he died of natural causes," said Dan.

"I'll be there as soon as I can." She hung up and returned to the table, flopping hard on the stool. Her head dropped onto the table. With her face in her hands, she cried, "No. No. No." She lifted her head and began sobbing, "Dad's dead."

Stunned, the group went silent. They all knew Bruce was recovering from a heart attack and had suffered from several chronic conditions. Still, no one expected the end to come so soon.

"Sorry to ruin our big night," said Meg.

"Nothing could ruin tonight. Let me take you to your Dad's place. We'll find out what's going on."

Jansen and Briggs paid and were ready to go when Larson walked over. "Jansen, I want you to follow-up on the death. Right now, you and Briggs should go home. You don't want to be blowing beer breath at the scene. Tomorrow morning is soon enough."

Larson led Meg from the pub to his car, closed the door, then stood outside while he called and talked to the watch commander.

"What did you find out?" Meg asked.

"It was assisted suicide. Bruce used the Death with Dignity Act to get the drugs to end his life. It was pre-approved months ago."

"Can't be. He never said a thing to me." She began crying again.

Larson reached over and put his hand on her shoulder. "It'll be okay, Babe. Hang in there." While Meg was wiping away her tears, Larson called Jansen. "It was assisted suicide with his brother at Bruce's side. Talk to Dan. Don't do a report unless something feels off."

"Will do, Chief," Jansen said.

"It's about time you showed a little respect for my stripes, Jansen."

"In your dreams," she said, constantly poking each other, even in the darkest moments.

Larson hung up, turned to Meg, and said, "I'm here for you. You won't go through this alone. We're family. Or soon will be."

"We are family," she confirmed. "I love you. And I need you now more than ever."

Larson smiled. A few minutes later, they pulled up in front of the building housing McQuillan's Books and Bruce's third-floor apartment.

They got out of the car just as a man in a black suit, white shirt, and dark tie wheeled a covered body onto the sidewalk.

"That's my dad," Meg said to the man who began loading Bruce's body into the hearse.

"Sorry for your loss," he said and handed her his card. "We'll take good care of him. Our funeral director will be in touch to explain the arrangements your father made."

She nodded, turned away, and buried her head in Larson's shoulder. "It'll be okay," he said.

Larson spotted Coroner Lisa Begley exiting the building. "Meg, let me talk to Dr. Begley for a minute."

"Lisa, how are you?" Larson asked.

"I was in the middle of a good movie, very relaxed when the call came in. But interruptions 24 hours a day is normal."

Larson ignored the complaint. "Anything off with McQuillan's death?"

"By the book," said Begley. "Good night, Larson."

"What have you been drinking?" she asked.

"Jamaican Me Pumpkin IPA," he said. "I was out with Jansen, Briggs, and Meg when we got the call."

"What's the occasion?" asked Begley.

"We were celebrating. I had just proposed to Meg McQuillan, the deceased's daughter. She accepted."

"Hot damn," said Begley. "I was wondering when you would get back on the horse."

"Yes, I finally saddled up, as painful as it has been. Do me a big favor, Lisa. Please keep it to yourself for now."

"My lips are sealed," she said, moving her fingers over her lips as if zipping them closed.

2

Jansen called Dan McQuillan the following day to discuss the details of Bruce's death. He picked up on the first ring.

"This is Detective Kim Jansen with the Portland Police Bureau."

"I know who you are," he said in a friendly voice. "Meg's best friend. Meg told me about Mark's proposal. I wish Bruce had lived one day longer. He would have relished knowing Meg was engaged."

"Dan, can you tell me what happened?"

"On top of Bruce's heart condition and chronic lung disease, he recently got a diagnosis of lung cancer that had spread. The doctor gave him three to six months to live. After that, he decided it would be less painful to call it quits. He didn't want Meg to suffer through months of watching him decline. I promised not to tell her." He didn't share Bruce's whispered secret. That could never happen, especially with a cop.

Jansen had no more questions. Nothing appeared to be out of the ordinary. The law clearly spelled out the requirements for choosing death on your own timetable.

Dan said Bruce would be cremated, his remains placed in a concrete vault, and buried in the same plot as his wife, Joan. She had died a decade earlier of ovarian cancer. The burial would be in Mt. Calvary Catholic Cemetery. Bruce didn't want a funeral, he said. Instead, a memorial would be held at McQuillan's Books for long-standing customers and friends. Dan would play bagpipes at the memorial, per Bruce's request.

When her phone showed a call from Meg, Jansen told Dan she had to take it and thanked him for his help. "See you at the memorial," she said and hung up.

CHAPTER 9

Jansen

1

"Nothing is easy, is it, Briggs? We go for beers with Mark, watch him propose, hear Meg agree to be his wife, then witness her meltdown over her father's death—all in 30 minutes.

"A bizarre evening. And we never got to discuss my job offer."

"I think you should accept it. I'll retire, become a housewife, and do something useful like knit scarves."

"Really?"

Jansen gave him a playful punch in the arm. "Forget it, buster. You know I don't cook, don't wash, don't iron, and hate to clean, let alone make a bed. You'll have to be in charge of bed-making." They both laughed. "And unfortunately, I never learned to knit."

"Jansen, what did you do today?"

"Bruce McQuillan's death was my primary focus, wrapping up the coroner's report and helping Meg with a few details for the memorial. Larson and I will be posted as official police bureau honor guards. Chief Morgan is allowing it, based on generations of McQuillans helping local cops with book theft cases and donating thousands to police charities."

"You'll look very sharp in your dress uniform."

"Assuming it still fits."

"Are you looking for a compliment about your slim body and tight ass?" said Briggs.

She smiled.

"Tell me about the job offer."

"The C-14 Foundation has a 14-person advisory board. Seven men and seven women. One less now with the death of Ian Reid, who also was C-14's vet. I'll take over his practice but won't replace him as a member. They didn't say who will do that."

"What does the C stand for?"

"Cardinal. Jed said he was 14 when he saw his first cardinal and fell in love with the color red; it reminds him of blood. I must have given him an odd look because he reminded me that he's a heart surgeon. Other members of the group also love vibrant red birds. And get this, his wife is a redhead. Do you think it's a coincidence that he fell in love with a red bird when he was a horny teen and married a redhead? A little strange. Did I mention that the C-14 members call themselves the Red Flock? I'm okay with the eccentricities of millionaires. However, I'm not comfortable with them importing endangered birds. And my job would be to manage the care for each member's collection of rare live birds and keep them that way."

"What's the problem?" Jansen asked.

"They claim to work closely with U.S. federal agencies and foreign counterparts to ensure the Foundation is within the law. I don't believe it because enforcement agencies would never allow rare birds to be removed from their native countries."

"Okay," said Jansen. "I'll do a background check on the Foundation tomorrow. In the meantime, let's assume all is on the up and up. Let's celebrate. You can show your bed-making skills." She grabbed his hand and headed upstairs.

2

Jansen had just instructed the department's researcher to check out the C-14 Foundation and Jed Miller when a sergeant manning the front desk buzzed her desk phone. "You've got a Fed here who says she has questions for you. What have you done, now?"

"I'd like to know, too. Send her up." Jansen knew her visitor was Betty Perez. She and Betty, long-time friends, had worked as rookie Portland street cops. Betty was immediately bored and took classes to get into law school. The cost of college, even with a few scholarships, was prohibitive until an FBI recruiter got hold of her. She got the brass ring based on interviews, high aptitude scores, and her fluency in Spanish and Russian—her father was Russian. The government paid a full scholarship to law school in exchange for a 10-year commitment to the Bureau. When she graduated, they assigned her to international enforcement cases.

"Betty, my sister, how the hell are you?" They fist-bumped, then hugged.

"Jansen, you look as fresh as ever. Not sure how you manage it after what you've been through the past couple of years. You'll always be my role model for bravery and pluck."

"You always were good with words. Plucky. Full of pluck. Yep, that's me, a dogged fighter. Lately, I'm the fighter getting knocked to the canvas."

"I never thought I would say this, but your job is more interesting than mine," said Perez. "Who knew so much agent work involved sitting on your butt, doing paperwork?"

"Don't delude yourself," said Jansen. "If we stacked our paper piles next to each other, I'll bet mine would be higher."

"You sound bored to death, like me. But, lucky for you, I have something to perk you up," said Perez. "Can we talk someplace private?"

"Follow me."

Jansen led Perez into the police bureau's new conference room. "Sit down, Betty. Let me make you a latte."

"A latte machine?" said Perez, rolling her eyes. "Sure. If you can make one with a heart on it, I'll see if I can get you a job as a barista in our break room."

"Fuck you very much, Perez," she said, laughing. When she had finished their drinks, they settled into the conference room's plush leather chairs.

"What's up?"

"Your husband has unwittingly put himself in the middle of a major investigation into a global poaching ring. He hasn't done anything wrong. But the people who want to hire him illegally import endangered birds for amusement."

Jansen's hand dropped so hard that coffee jumped out of the cup onto the table. She didn't notice the spill. Instead, her eyes locked on Perez, waiting for more.

"This is off the record. Need-to-know," said Betty. "That okay with you?"

"Of course," said Jansen, her jaw tightening, her mouth forming a tight line.

"Our undercover officers observed Jim drive onto the Miller Estate in Portland's West Hills, where Jed Miller greeted him before they disappeared into the house for more than an hour. We know Jim was there to interview for a job as C-14's new veterinarian. The previous veterinarian, a retired guy around 75, died of a heart attack. They desperately need a new vet to care for their birds and manage the transfer of rare birds to the Millers for distribution to their members."

"I knew the job was too good to be true. Jim said they offered him a $50,000 signing bonus and six figures for part-time work."

Jansen looked down, saw the coffee spill, got up to get a paper towel, and wiped up the mess. She crumpled the towel into a ball and tossed it across the room into a wastebasket.

"Nice shot," said Perez.

"What does all this mean for Jim and me?"

"Jim, along with another informant we just recruited, can help us break this case wide open. The C-14 Foundation members are using their buying power to scoop up bird species headed for extinction. We have to stop them and do it fast."

"How do they operate?"

"The Millers have made trips all over Mexico and Central and South America, meeting with government officials in charge of wildlife preservation. They offer millions of dollars to support their anti-poaching and forest protection programs. The quid pro quo is to fulfill requests from C-14 members for rare birds. The C-14 members pay a million yearly for membership and bonus amounts when their bird request is filled. The poachers get $100,000 per bird, some of which they divvy among locals as bribes. The bosses probably take most of it."

"And you want Jim to accept the job, embed himself, and wear a wire?"

"You were always intuitive," said Perez, winking.

"There you go with your big words and sweet talk. Must be why I love you, Betty."

Jansen told Perez she had just begun her own background check on C-14 when Perez arrived. "Jim said he was uncomfortable with their explanation of how they got rare birds. They claimed to be rescuing them to preserve the species. Jim said that U.S. and international laws make it clear an endangered species must never leave its native country or habitat."

"Smart man," said Perez.

"He is, but don't tell him that. His ego is already too big."

"An ego to match his size," Perez said, smiling. "I know. We've gotta bring these guys down to Earth from time to time. Even the big ones."

"One more thing," Perez added. "Our operation has identified a spider web of organized crime and couriers acting as middlemen. There are dangers for an informant."

"I understand," said Jansen. "I think you can count on Jim to help. I'll talk to him tonight and call you can call in the morning."

"You're a peach," said Perez.

"There you go again with that silver tongue. I'll allow it if you don't let any other detectives hear you."

"I could call you a Wooden Shoe Blue."

"Then I would have to kill you," said Jansen. "Give me one more hug and get out of here."

They opened the door. Perez shouted, "I know you said no, but please consider joining the Bureau. More money and prestige than being a lowly detective."

Jansen smiled, winked, and whispered, "Go fuck yourself, Perez. First, the FBI has no latte machines or glove-soft leather conference room chairs. Second, my fellow detectives are my BFFs. I'm here for life."

"Nice fairy tale," Perez whispered.

"Didn't think you'd buy it. I need to hit the lottery for a few million, then retire."

CHAPTER 10

Dan

1

The least he could do for Bruce was to fulfill his request for a bagpipe tribute to open the memorial at McQuillan's Books. He was rusty. He hadn't played in 20 years but would do it for family honor and respect for his brother's wishes. Tears welled in his eyes. He already missed him. Dan took a deep breath, let it out, and reviewed the memorial checklist Bruce had prepared.

Bruce's closest friends, most of them Scots, had lined up along the sidewalk in front of the store. A dozen long-time customers were ready to join the procession. It was a few minutes before 5 pm and sunset, the time Bruce had set for the tribute to begin.

Although "Amazing Grace" was the most requested song for bagpipers at funerals and memorials, Bruce had asked that Dan play "Scotland, the Brave." Dan and two drummers would start at the end of the block and march to the store's open double front door and halt. As they continued to play, a member of the procession would walk forward and hand the urn with Bruce's cremated remains to Meg, who would place it on the table next to Bruce's photo.

Dan looked at his watch. Two minutes.

He walked to the store entrance and stepped inside. Meg looked at him, tears wetting her cheeks. "Are you ready?" he asked.

"I'll never get used to losing Dad."

"You're not alone," Dan reminded her, looking at Mark Larson and Kim Jansen, standing erect in their dress blues. They flanked the table. Dan shook hands with each of them. "Thanks for organizing the police tribute. Bruce would be proud." Jansen and Larson nodded solemnly.

Dan patted Meg's shoulder. "The formal part will be over soon, and we'll get to Bruce's favorite—a tribute with good Scotch whiskey."

Dan walked out the door to the waiting procession. He picked up his bagpipes. He turned and yelled, "Let's do it."

When the mourners reached the door, a friend holding Bruce's remains walked forward and handed them to Meg, who set them on a table. At the same moment, a loud crack echoed through the downtown canyon of buildings, and the porcelain container holding Bruce's ashes exploded. Shrapnel sprayed everyone within 10 feet.

"Everyone down," Larson commanded. He and Jansen got on their hands and knees, carefully pushing aside glass and urn shards as they crawled to other victims. The gun blast had been so powerful it had sent shrapnel through a nearby window, creating its own blast area.

"You should go to Meg," Jansen said.

Larson looked toward the table where Meg had been standing. Meg's face was a mass of blood. Her eye appeared damaged. Larson ran across the room, ignoring a piece of urn that had embedded in his hand, numbing it. All he wanted to do was get to her as fast as possible. He had to save her. He couldn't let her die like he let Helen.

Jansen looked around and assessed the damage. Her own shoulder was bloody. Jim Briggs had pulled a piece of glass from his forearm and was applying pressure with his shirt. Dan's neck was bleeding, and he appeared to be unconscious. Other mourners had sustained minor injuries. Bruce's ashes covered everything close to the point of impact.

Jansen pulled out her radio and called the station. "We have an 11-99, two officers and ten civilians wounded, active shooter nearby. Possibly from the rooftop. Proceed with extreme caution."

2

Five minutes later, the sound of police cars and ambulances filled the downtown. A SWAT team, led by Lt. Bull Harrison, Jansen's former patrol sergeant, arrived at the scene. Harrison and his men took cover as they looked toward the rooftops. Harrison radioed his team members to enter three nearby buildings and a parking garage in search of the shooter.

Briggs found a first aid kit and he and Jansen began applying bandages to victims and pressure to wounds. She listened to her radio as search sites were cleared. When the SWAT team sweep of the area was finished, Lt. Harrison signaled the all-clear. "Negative contact with a shooter."

With the immediate threat over, several members of Larson's detective squad and paramedics flooded the store.

The paramedics quickly assessed the injuries and zeroed in on Dan's neck wounds and Meg's bloody face. While working to stem Meg's bleeding, Larson identified himself and informed the paramedic he would ride in the ambulance with Meg to the hospital. He was holding a towel over his own hand to staunch the bleeding. "Let me look at that," a second paramedic said.

"I'll be okay until I get to the hospital. The most important thing is to take this woman there ASAP." He didn't tell them she was the love of his life—his future wife.

"Jansen, I'm going to the hospital with Meg," said Larson. "I'm putting you in charge of the investigation. First, we need to find the shooter, which means we need to figure out a motive and who the target was."

"That's the hell of it, Larson," said Jansen. "Anyone here could have been the target. You and I no doubt have plenty of enemies. But why would someone shoot at Dan or Meg?"

"Was Bruce the target?" asked Larson. "They ruined his memorial and left his remains on the bookstore floor. A vendetta? A creditor owed money? Before you do anything, get your arm checked out. You're bleeding like a stuck pig."

Jansen looked at the sleeve of her uniform jacket and saw it was soaked with blood. She put her hand over the wound just as a paramedic reached her. "We need to get you to the hospital," he said.

"Can't," she said. "See this mess? I'm the investigating officer in charge."

The paramedic took off her jacket and assessed the wound. "A flesh wound," he said. "I'll get you bandaged up, but you'll need to get it checked out again later.

With her arm bandaged, she huddled with Harrison. He held up a plastic bag with a shell casing. "We've got a serious shooter," he said. "This is .600 Nitro Express casing. It's powerful enough to bring down a charging rhino," he said. "We found scuff marks on the roof, evidence a tripod was used to stabilize the gun. It must have been a big mother."

"Thanks, Bull," she said. "I'll get the forensics team up there."

The shooter must have meant the shot as a warning, Jansen thought. So who was it for and why?

CHAPTER 11

Lexi

1

Lexi Miller broke down her rifle, then wrapped the pieces in her yoga mat—one more Portlander on her way to an end-of-day workout. When she arrived at her car six blocks from McQuillan's, she casually opened the back and put her mat and rifle inside. She was on her way home by the time the first sirens sounded.

Did Dan McQuillan get her message not to screw with the price? Watching Bruce's urn explode, sending up a cloud of his remains, should be enough to convince Dan what was at stake.

If he persisted in his effort to squeeze the Millers for more money, Lexi had devised an alternate plan: pretend to accept the higher price, then—if necessary—take out Dan, secure the books, and send the proceeds to Meg McQuillan. Lexi had no intention of cheating Meg out of her inheritance. On the contrary, based on the dilapidated condition of McQuillan's Books, the money would be a welcome reprieve from bankruptcy and the store's closure. Bruce McQuillan had been honest, she thought, about the state of his business and how important the deal was for Meg's future. Unfortunately, with Bruce dead, his greedy brother was driving the deal.

When Lexi got home, she took the rifle to her wing of the house and set it on a workbench she used to maintain her weapons. A few minutes later, Jed arrived home from the hospital after eight hours of heart surgeries and texted her, "In the kitchen having a cup of coffee. Join me."

"On my way," she texted back.

2

"Hi, sweetheart," said Lexi, as she walked into the kitchen and kissed Jed. He was slumped on a stool, drinking a glass of wine. "What happened? I thought you were having coffee."

"I decided I needed something more. Today was a seesaw. I saved an obese woman with a severely enlarged heart, then lost a young, healthy athlete with a heart valve defect. I'm still in shock. The athlete apparently suffered a fatal stroke. A rare, rare thing. And it happened to *me*—on *my* watch. Think about how his family will suffer for the rest of their lives."

Lexi hugged him. "I'm sure you did your best."

"Always. And my best almost always saves my patients, but not this time. Facing his family was like getting knocked to the canvas in a prize fight. When I feel like that, I don't want to get up. I want to close my eyes and pretend I'm someplace else, like Bali, snorkeling in a tropical lagoon."

"You have one thing to look forward to. Tonight's the wine-tasting event at Byrne Vineyards. I'm curious to see what prison did to that beautiful man."

Jed brightened. "I think the judge did the right thing, giving him a light sentence," said Jed. "Colin defied the odds and created a successful winery despite his father's brutality, which cost him an eye as a kid. Sending him to prison was punishing him for what his father did."

"He did conspire to steal rare books and a guard was injured during the theft," Lexi minded Jed. She looked at her watch. "We've got just enough time for a catnap, dress, and make it to Colin's homecoming by eight," Lexi said.

"How was your day?" Jed asked.

"Uneventful. I painted in the morning, attended a yoga class after lunch, then spent an hour at Andy's Firing Pen shooting the big gun. It's such a beautiful piece and so powerful. It would be a shame to only use it on big game hunts."

And by the way, she thought, I injured a dozen people. Jed put up with her obsession over Audubon's work, but she knew she had gone over top and was too embarrassed to admit what she had done.

"I'll see you in an hour, and we'll head to Byrne Vineyards."

"Did you hear all the sirens on your way home?" asked Jed.

"I turned on the radio to find out what it was but couldn't find any news reports."

"I checked Chuck Grayson's UrbanStreetPDX blog to see if he had a new post," said Jed. "So far, just one sentence to alert readers to gunfire downtown and a police response."

"We'll know soon enough," said Lexi. "Go get that nap." Then, as he turned, she slapped him on the bottom. "Cute butt."

"Maybe I should skip the nap so you can join me in the shower," he said.

"Nice try," she said, giving him one more kiss before heading to her room.

3

Lexi went to her closet to pick out her party outfit. Lexi and Jed loved Byrne's highly-rated red wines but also loved that he was a birding fanatic. Byrne had built a life list of 5,000 birds. He also launched Wine Hawks, Inc, a service that placed hawks and falcons in vineyards to protect vines against grape-damaging birds. The Millers had helped plan and finance the business in exchange for 49 percent of the stock. Byrne and Jed also served on the Portland Audubon Society Board of Directors.

Lexi and Jed had proposed Colin Byrne as C-14's replacement for Ian Reid. Byrne won easy approval from other members, most of them his friends. They were sure he would accept the membership offer.

4

Lexi spotted Byrne among the crowd of friends and wine club members who welcomed him back after his imprisonment. "Colin," Lexi called. He turned, excused himself from a small group of wine, and headed her way.

"Lexi, you're as beautiful as ever," said Colin, wrapping her in a hug. "You know how much I love that red hair."

"Is that all?" said Lexi, feigning a pout.

She kissed him and parted. "And you are forever the handsome one-eyed pirate," she said, referring to the black patch over his eye. Byrne was Black Irish, distinguished by wavy jet-black hair, pale skin, and bright blue eyes.

"You look as fit as ever," said Lexi, looking him up and down.

"Not much to do in jail but exercise," he said. "Every meal was cafeteria food. And, of course, no wine to enhance the flavor." Lexi laughed. "And I was in a minimum-security facility known as a country club. Don't believe it. God help hardened criminals living in single cells for life."

"Colin, good to see you," said Jed, joining them and pulling him into a hug. "I missed you, my friend."

After a minute or two of small talk, Jed looked around furtively and moved closer to Colin. "I know you need to circulate, so we'll only take a minute. The Red Flock has voted to invite you to join the C-14 Foundation."

A flush of excitement turned Colin's white skin a light shade of red. "That would be an honor," said Colin.

"Great news," said Lexi, hugging Colin again. She and Jed raised a glass to Colin and said, "Here's to flying free."

"You can say that again," said Colin, lifting his glass.

As they walked away, Lexi said, "That went well."

"I hate to say it," said Jed. "I think prison agreed with him. He looks great."

"Prison might be good for you," Lexi said, "if it got that tummy of yours flatter and tighter."

"Ouch," he said.

"Don't even think about it," said Lexi, warning Jed against retaliating with his own comment about her belly fat and less-than-perky tits.

Jed shook his head vigorously and said, "would I make disparaging remarks about the love of my life—my little Cherry-Throated Tanager?" They laughed.

"Colin served less than a year in prison," said Lexi, frowning. "How would we cope in prison for 10 years? We'll be ruined if the Feds ever catch on to our preservation program. Our life will be over. I would kill myself before going to prison."

"Don't be ridiculous," said Jed. "Our hearts are pure."

"Tell that to the FBI," said Lexi.

Jed cocked his head. "You seem uneasy. You're having doubts about our rare bird acquisition program and have been talking a lot of doom and gloom the past few weeks. What's bothering you?"

Lexi took a long drink of Byrne Vineyards Pinot Noir and said, "I feel like we're so close to achieving our dreams. What if it all goes to hell?"

"Have some more wine. You worry too much."

They waved at Colin to get his attention, then raised their glasses and silently mouthed, "Welcome home." Colin smiled and raised his glass.

CHAPTER 12

Jed

1

On the drive home, Lexi looked at her phone. A text alerted her to a new post on the UrbanStreetPDX blog. The headline read, *Bullet Blows Up Beloved Bookman's Memorial, A Dozen Injured.* A bulletin followed.

By Chuck Grayson, Editor

An unidentified sniper fired at the procession carrying the cremated remains of Bruce McQuillan, owner of McQuillan's Books, injuring two police detectives and bystanders. At least a dozen mourners suffered injuries, police report.

The bullet hit the porcelain urn with McQuillan's remains. Witnesses said it exploded like a grenade, wounding everyone standing within a 10-foot radius.

According to one observer at the scene, McQuillan's ashes sprayed across the floor and onto nearby bookshelves.

The shrapnel hit Chief Detective Mark Larson and Detective Kim Jansen, who were attending as a police honor guard. Meg McQuillan, the dead man's daughter, had significant facial injuries and may lose an eye. Dan McQuillan, Bruce's brother, also suffered injuries from the flying pieces of porcelain. Veterinarian Jim Briggs, Det. Jansen's husband, suffered an arm wound.

"Whoever did this is a monster," Chief Larson said, his arm bandaged from a deep wound. "What kind of person tries to kill people at a memorial? Bruce McQuillan was a good man whose family supported our community and the police department for decades. Know that we will track down and apprehend the perpetrator. They will pay dearly."

The shooting took place at sunset during a procession of mourners, led by McQuillan's Scottish friends, who played drums, and his brother Dan, who played bagpipes in Bruce's honor.

A source close to the investigation said police are unsure who the sniper was targeting. More to come as the police investigation unfolds.

"What are you reading?" asked Jed.

"Someone fired a bullet at the people gathered for Bruce McQuillan's memorial earlier this evening. The police are investigating. They apparently have no suspects or motives. Nor do they know who the target was. Early days, according to Chuck Grayson's Urban Street PDX blog.

"That's terrible. Who the hell would do something like that?" His comment was like a slap in the face.

Lexi's stomach convulsed and her chest tightened. She didn't have the heart to tell Jed she was the shooter. That she had not intended to hurt anyone. Now, she felt shame for letting her dream of owning *The Birds of America* get out of hand. No one was supposed to get hurt.

"Got your message," said a text on her phone. She had silenced it so it wouldn't alert Jed to more bulletins. This one was from Dan McQuillan. "It was a shitty move. It may have cost you an extra million dollars."

Lexi's heart sank.

"Meet me tomorrow at Andy's Firing Pen at 10 a.m. sharp," McQuillan wrote. "Let's get this deal done. Remember, the price isn't finalized. And with today's display of stupidity, you're in no position to negotiate."

Lexi's had really screwed up. She and Jed had already agreed to pay the higher price. There was no need to shoot anyone or even threaten them. Instead, charges of attempted murder of police officers, assault with a deadly weapon, and conspiracy to buy stolen property would jail her for decades. Who knows what else? How much sympathy would a jury give her—a wealthy woman so desperate to own rare books that she nearly kills a dozen people?

Dan

2

Dan McQuillan looked in the mirror and saw a man with bandages covering half his face. The ER doctor needed 16 stitches to close one wound and had treated a half dozen smaller cuts and bruises from fragment impacts. His face resembled the moon's cratered surface. Thank God Bruce wasn't alive to witness how Dan had flubbed *The Birds of America* sale. And the deal still wasn't done.

Dan wanted to strangle Lexi Miller. In his mind, he imagined her head as a target in his sniper rifle sights. A gentle squeeze of the trigger from 1000 yards would turn her bird brain into a spray of red mist, like the terrorists he killed in the Middle East. He never regretted a single shot or lost sleep over his kills. Fellow soldiers were in awe of his skill with a rifle. Would taking out Lexi Miller be bothersome? Probably not. He would need to find another buyer for the Audubon books. After getting the money and squaring with his niece, Meg, he had no intention of hanging around to co-manage the nearly dead bookstore.

His grandfather had a good idea during The Depression to leverage the bookstore as a job bank for generations to come. Granddad figured that none would end up hobos or living in a cardboard box. He was right. But that was then and this was now. Dan didn't have to think twice about giving Meg his half of the store. She could do whatever she wanted. Selling dusty used books by the bag for 50 cents each would kill anyone's spirit. Meg deserved more.

Dan snapped out of the daydream, went to the closet, picked up one of four Audubon volumes, and laid it on the carpet. Turning the pages, he realized he was thumbing through a book worth millions of dollars. The photos of the birds were beautiful. Audubon was clearly a gifted artist. But pretty bird pictures didn't interest him.

Dan closed the book, placed it back in a locked cabinet he had purchased online to store them, and headed to bed. Tomorrow he could settle on a price, take a significant down payment, and deliver the first of the four-volume set. Delivering one book would be a tease. The value was in the entire set, not one volume. He knew Lexi—given her wealth and his husband's attempt to buy the books at auction for over $11 million—would get all four, or die trying,

Lexi

3

"I'm out of here," said Jed, slugging down the last gulp of coffee, his third cup of the morning. "Got two very complicated surgeries today. I won't be home early. I hope today is better than yesterday. Before I go, give me a party update."

"Bill Masterson is coming over to meet his new parrot companion tomorrow," said Lexi. "I've got 100 percent RSVPs, including Colin Byrne, for this week's Red Flock gathering."

"You look uneasy," said Jed, pulling her in close. He held her face with his hands. "Are you worried about your parrot painting?"

"Just anxious to finalize the deal with Dan McQuillan to buy *Birds*. We'll meet at 10 a.m. at Andy's Firing Pen to conclude the details."

"Lexi, you're the best. In a few days, we'll have the complete set. We might even display it at a future meeting of the Flock." Lexi was silent.

"Gotta go," he said as he raced out the door, climbed into his red SUV, and raced off to the hospital.

Lexi loaded her rifle into her car, then texted Dan she was on her way to Andy's.

"I'll be there," he responded. "Pissed off and armed with my big gun."

CHAPTER 13

Dan

Dan McQuillan loaded up one of the four *The Birds of America* volumes and placed it in the trunk of his car, along with his sniper rifle. The military prohibited the removal of government property, including weapons of war, after a person's discharge. His commanding officer ignored the regulation and gave the rifle to Dan as a keepsake. "You earned it," he said. His commander figured it needed retiring the same way teams retire the number of legendary sports figures. "No one is going to get your gun," he told Dan. "You got the kills for your country."

Dan knew that killing a record number of the enemy wasn't like hitting a record number of home runs. As brutal as it might sound to a civilian with no military experience, killing is what soldiers are trained for. Dan's conscience was clear. Unlike super athletes, snipers couldn't put a trophy on their mantle to show off.

"Hey, fellah, you're new around here?" asked Andy.

"Yep, visiting and helping my brother," said Dan.

"Not to be nosy, but what happened to your face?" Dan had purposely pulled off the bandages so Lexi could see the damage she had caused.

"You heard about that shooting yesterday at McQuillan's Books?"

"Hell, yes. The news was filled with it last night."

"I was leading the memorial for my brother, Bruce McQuillan. We had just set down Bruce's ashes when the bullet crashed into the container holding his remains."

"What a lousy thing for someone to do," said Andy.

"I agree. I'm Dan McQuillan, Bruce's younger brother."

They shook hands. "Are you the same Dan McQuillan as the Army's top sniper during the Vietnam War?"

"That'd be me. And this is the friend I carried with me on those missions." Dan unpacked the gun and lifted it up on the counter. Andy caressed the long barrel like he would a woman's soft arm—slowly and gently.

"You're what the military calls a secret warrior. They're the folks asked to go where no one else would, doing what needed to be done, no questions asked."

"You want to know what brings me to Andy's Firing Pen?"

"Lexi told me to expect a guy named Dan."

"Bruce and Lexi go way back," said Dan, lying. *Way back* was six months when they hatched the Audubon deal. "Turns out Lexi and I both like big guns. I promised to show her mine, and she said she would show me hers." Dan raised his eyebrows. Dan smiled.

"I better let you two go at it. Lexi has been here 10 minutes and is not known for her patience."

Dan walked out a backdoor into the firing range. A few people were shooting, but it was quieter than usual for a firing range. He spotted Lexi and sauntered toward her. They had never met. And he didn't like her, especially after yesterday's stunt at Bruce's memorial.

Lexi had been looking for a young man. Instead, an old man with a long gray ponytail, shorts, sandals, and a Hawaiian shirt was approaching. He looked like a beach bum, a guy heading for a luau rather than a shootout.

"You're Dan?"

"Who'd you expect?"

"Someone younger."

"Don't let the cover of this dusty book fool you."

Lexi half smiled.

Dan unpacked his sniper rifle, held it up, and said in a low voice, "This baby has blown away dozens of men who never knew what hit them. Ripped their heads clean off. The same could happen to you."

Lexi's mouth dropped open. Dan looked out the corner of his eye to gauge her reaction. Of course, any woman who hunted big game wouldn't be intimidated. Still, his reputation as a sniper—at least among ex-military—allowed for some swagger. Lexi's jaw tightened. Fear wasn't in her vocabulary. "Let's shoot," she said, aiming her elephant gun toward a target 250 yards out.

For the next 10 minutes, Dan and Lexi traded shots at targets. Their guns sounded like ship cannons blasting their enemies as they moved alongside each other. Lexi scowled at Dan before she fired each shot. Dan squinted as if sighting an enemy combatant. They traded shots, squeezing out anger with each bullet.

Stunned by the intensity of the battle, other range shooters put down their weapons and gawked at the display of power.

"Alright," said Lexi. "You've made your point. I'm sorry about what happened yesterday. I meant no disrespect to your brother. I didn't want anyone to get hurt."

"Let's move on," said Dan. "Here's the deal. Take it or leave it: $5 million."

"Not a penny more than $4 million," Lexi countered.

Dan looked away into the distance. Is she bluffing? Would the sale die over a million dollars when her husband at the auction had bid twice what Dan wanted? He would have to find another buyer if she walked away from the deal. Should he ask for $4.5 million? What was the point?

"You've got yourself a pretty set of bird books," said Dan.

Lexi put her gun down, walked over to Dan, and hugged him.

Not what he expected.

She let go and said, "First, I want to make sure you have them."

"Better yet, as a matter of good faith, I've brought one volume. Take it home and look it over. If you're satisfied, you'll need to wire the money by the end of the day tomorrow." They shook hands.

"A powerful woman," Dan thought, the strength of her grip surprising him, as did the fury of her shooting.

They silently packed their guns and headed out to the parking lot. Their audience looked away, settling back into their shooting lanes.

"Impressive shooting today," said Andy. "You two ought to form a team."

"Not my type," Dan said. "Too noisy."

Lexi shot him a look that could kill.

When they got to Dan's car, he popped the trunk and moved the Audubon book to Lexi's car. She closed the lid.

"Do we have a deal?" asked Dan, reconfirming the terms.

"We do," said Lexi. "You'll have the money as promised, assuming the goods check out."

"When I've confirmed the transaction, I'll bring the other books to your place tomorrow. Will that work?"

"I'll text directions when everything is verified," said Lexi.

"You're a damn good shot," said Dan. "You would have made a good Army sniper."

"Thanks," said Lexi. "I'll accept the compliment. Not sure I would how I would feel about killing people."

"Based on yesterday's shooting demonstration, you would be fine."

"Bye," said Lexi, who climbed into her car and drove away. When she was out of sight, she pulled over, drummed on the steering wheel, and did a dance with her hands.

Standing in the parking lot of Andy's, Dan performed his own dance, the Highland Fling, his ponytail swinging like a galloping horse.

CHAPTER 14

Jansen

1

Chief Detective Larson stood in front of his assembled detectives, his wounded hand in a sling.

"We're getting the usual political pressure to find the memorial shooter. Ignore it. I'll deal with the bureaucrats. We've got a shooter out there who was either firing a warning shot or had poor aim. We need to find the gun, the motive, and the suspect. In other words, we've got nothing except the bullet caliber fired. Jansen will be leading the investigation."

"Thanks, Chief," said Jansen, moving to the front of the room as Larson turned and walked back to his office.

"Munson, you call gun shops to see if they have had any recent sales of Nitro ammo or weapons that use that load," said Jansen. "You're a pro. You know the routine." Munson smiled at the compliment, then said, "Thanks for the confidence, Junior Detective Jansen." With nine years more detective experience, Alice Munson made it clear to everyone that she thought she should be in charge. Jansen ignored the dig.

"Berenson, you call Andy's Firing Pen and ask him about big gun shooters who frequent his range.

"Millbrook, I want you to interview Dan McQuillan, one of our victims and Bruce's brother. He's new to Portland. Dig into his background. I'm going back to interview Meg McQuillan. What you may not know is that Larson is engaged to Meg. Just happened. I wouldn't mention it to him. I think he intended to keep it a secret for a while longer. However, I feel you need to know why he's taking a less active role in this investigation. There's a conflict of interest, plus, because of Meg's extensive injuries, we can expect him to be distracted. Don't let that distract *you*. Whoever was the target could end up dead unless we find the shooter first."

Jansen scanned the room for questions.

"Who's looking into suspects aimed at you or Larson?" asked Munson.

"Larson and I will focus on anyone we've put away who might want payback. The list could be long."

"I know one," said Munson.

Jansen cocked her head, waiting for the name.

"Colin Byrne, the millionaire wine guy you put in jail last year," she said. "Remember him? He's out of jail."

"Munson, as lazy as you are, you get credit for stimulating your bird brain and coming up with Byrne. Good thinking. Keep it up, and you could be a real detective one day. I see hope for you."

Munson flipped her off and said, "You're welcome."

Jansen didn't see Byrne as a suspect. Yes, she had put Byrne away. But he admitted he deserved it. And he got a light sentence, thanks to her. The rare books he conspired to steal from the Portland Central Library resulted in a security guard suffering a severe wound during the break-in. The victim's blood-stained a book from Edward S. Curtis' *The North American Indian*, a 20-volume set worth $3 million. The district attorney agreed to give Byrne the lighter sentence when Jansen got Byrne to pay for restoration of the book.

2

Jansen drove to the crime scene, ducked under the yellow tape blocking the entrance to McQuillan's Books, and entered through the unlocked front doors. She spotted a shadowy figure near the front counter. Instinctively, Jansen put her hand on her gun. As her eyes adjusted, she saw it was one of the crime scene investigators. She flipped on the overhead lights, filling the room with crackles and flashes from the fluorescents.

"Working in the dark?" she asked Bob Matsui, chief crime scene investigator for the Portland Police Bureau.

"Hilarious, Jansen. Shutting down. I think we have everything."

"Anything to share?"

"We have another victim."

"What are you talking about? Who? Where are they?"

"William Shakespeare. The bullet lodged in the heart of William Shakespeare, or at least Shakespeare's *Sonnets*, a fine copy of the 154 poems he wrote in the 1600s."

"Are you trying to give me a heart attack?"

"Just having fun. I would much rather take pictures of damaged books than people who are wounded or dead. And I like Shakespeare—his plays and his poetry. My wife and I drive to Ashland every year for the Shakespeare Festival."

Jansen shook her head. "Don't know how you could do that. I'm sure it's clever and interesting, and the man was a genius, but it's not how I imagine spending my leisure time. Do you have anything else for me?"

"You already have the shell casing from the roof across the street. And the bullet pried from Shakespeare's heart." He held up a plastic bag with his find. "The shell casing ought to match the bullet fired yesterday. As Bull Harrison said, this ammo is used to take down big African game animals, so they don't get up. You don't want them getting pissed and taking a run at you."

"If it had hit any one of us, we would be dead or missing a limb," she said.

"You're right about that, Jansen. We also found an unloaded 18-shot Ruger American pistol on a shelf under the cash register. I imagine it was the owner's way of deterring robberies. We left it there." He looked around at the scene. "That's it. I'm out of here. My report will be on your desk in the morning."

"Thanks," said Jansen. "I'll lock up. I'm going to look around and see if I can get my head around a motive for the shooting."

When Matsui left, Jansen wandered around the front of the store, then worked her way to the office. Books and papers were piled everywhere. How does anyone run a business surrounded by a mess like this?

After lifting a few papers and opening filing cabinets, Jansen looked over and saw a message machine. The light was flashing. She walked over and hit the play button.

3

A robotic voice on the recording machine, obviously disguised, warned, "Give me the damn bird book, or next time I won't miss." The recording lasted a few seconds. Jansen couldn't determine if the voice was male or female.

What bird book was worth killing for?

A second message was from Bruce McQuillan's attorney. It was for Meg, requesting a meeting to read Bruce's will.

After replaying the warning, she speed-dialed Jim.

"Briggs, can you think of a bird book worth enough to make someone kill for it?" Briggs was okay with her abruptness. When on a case, she often called him, demanding information, like she was twisting a suspect's arm.

"Is there a prize for the correct answer?"

"Do you enjoy poking the bear when she's hungry? Just answer the damn question. I'm busy, and the clock's ticking. I just heard a message on McQuillan's answering machine that demands someone turn over a bird book or else?"

"Do you think the shooter left the message?" Briggs asked.

"That's my guess."

"Remember a year and a half ago when James Audubon's four-volume book, *The Birds of America* went missing from the Central Library's John Wilson Collections?"

"All the anesthesia and blood loss I suffered when I was stabbed last year has left gaps in my memory. I totally forgot about it. Remind me what happened."

"I think Munson and Berenson handled the case," he said. "It's in the Bureau's files. But Chuck Grayson blog, UrbanStreetPDX, has a more colorful account. Marc Stanfield, the curator of the library's rare book room, was the chief suspect. The library board was going to fire him but he failed to turn up at his disciplinary hearing. He disappeared without a trace, as did the books."

"What's the value?" asked Jansen.

"A set sold this past week for $12 million. It's one of the world's most valuable books."

Jansen whistled.

"Thanks, Briggs. See you at home tonight. Let's go for beer and barbecue at Southland Whiskey Kitchen."

"Sounds good to me."

"Gotta go."

When the books went missing, Meg McQuillan had been a librarian at the Central Library where Stanfield worked. She'll know more, Jansen thought.

Jansen headed to the hospital, where Meg rested while doctors monitored the injured eye for infection.

On her way to the hospital, Jansen called CSI Matsui and left a message for him to get the recording. "It's a key piece of evidence. Pick it up, stat. It's in McQuillan's office at the back of the store on the first floor."

CHAPTER 15

Meg

Meg sat up in bed, picked up a mirror on her nightstand, and brought it to her face. Despite the doctor's order not to remove the bandage or disturb the wounded eye, she pulled the tape free at the bottom and lifted it. She had to see the damage. No doubt Mark would back away from his marriage proposal like it was a rattlesnake.

"Oh no," she cried. The eye, swollen half shut, was blood-red and weepie. Stitches on her eyelid marked where a porcelain sliver from her father's exploded cremation urn had struck. Meg dropped the mirror and pushed herself down under the blanket.

There was a knock at her door. "Come in," she said, dread in her voice as if more bad news was coming her way. She peeked out from the covers.

"Meg. It's Kim. Can I come in?"

Meg saw her friend's face and burst into tears. Jansen walked to the bed, sat down, and held Meg for a minute. Then she grabbed Meg by the shoulders, pushed her back gently, looked her over, and said, "Larson is a sucker for girl pirates."

"You think?"

"Absolutely. It's one of Mark's fetishes. Even better if you had a peg leg."

"In other words, stop feeling sorry for myself. Be a fighter. Mark loves me."

"Bingo," said Jansen, who reached over and combed Meg's hair with her fingers. "A little makeup, and you'll be good as gold."

"I needed something to yank me out of my funk. This place is emporium of sadness, self-doubt, and dark thoughts."

"I understand," Jansen said, reminding Meg about her own lengthy recovery after being stabbed. "I hear Larson is going to take you home this afternoon."

"I'm happy to leave but dreading his reaction."

"He'll be fine. Love has a funny way of creating this magic glow that blinds a person to all our imperfections." Meg nodded.

"I need to ask you some questions. The mayor, the police chief, and the community are in an uproar over the shooting and the desecration of Bruce's remains. As the lead investigator, a blowtorch on my ass tells me to move fast and solve this crime. I would like to be here for a friend visit, but I need your help."

"It's okay. What do you need?"

Jansen pulled out her cell phone. "We found a voicemail message in the bookstore. Let me play it for you."

'Give me the damn bird book or else,' the mechanical voice demanded. A loud clunk followed, the sound of someone slamming down the phone.

"Oh my god," said Meg.

"What are they talking about?" Jansen asked. "What bird book could be worth killing over?"

Meg's mind scanned the shelves of McQuillan's rare book collection. Nothing came to mind.

"I know all the rare books we're holding," said Meg. "None deal with birding."

"Could Bruce have been involved in some deal for a rare bird book before he died?"

"I think I would have known about it. Dad and I talked every day. We shared every detail about the business and inventory." Or at least she thought so.

"Let me ask it another way. Is there a bird book that someone might treasure, something rare?"

Meg closed her eyes for half a minute as if searching her memory, fuzzed by anesthesia. "There is one," said Meg. "It's John James Audubon's *Birds of America*. Last week a copy sold at auction, but we had nothing to do with that."

"Any idea who bought it?"

"According to Chuck Grayson at UrbanStreetPDX, an anonymous buyer won the bidding."

"I can't see a connection to this case right off," said Jansen.

Meg knew of one more copy. The one Marc Stanfield stole. But he literally vanished before she could ask him about it. She didn't want to believe the rumors about Marc and repeatedly attempted to call and text him without a response.

When he didn't respond, she was sure he was ghosting her for another woman or was dead. She grieved for months but never told the police or anyone else about their affair. Then, six months later, Stanfield finally texted, 'Love and miss you. More later.' A week later, he called and apologized for his disappearing act.

Stanfield told her he had rented a studio apartment in rural Eastern Oregon after changing his name and appearance. Excited to have Stanfield back in her life, Meg drove to his place and resumed their affair. Then she met Mark Larson, a single cop with no baggage—as far as she could tell. Stanfield, realizing he was about to lose Meg, confessed he took the books and had delayed their sale until the police investigation ended. He said his cut would pay off the mortgage of the home his wife was living in and pay his daughter's college tuition. Stanfield said he and Meg would have plenty of money left over, even after giving his wife a monthly allowance. Meg wasn't buying it. Her ailing father and financial problems at McQuillan's were all the baggage she could carry. She didn't need Stanfield's.

"I love you but can't be part of your life. You need to return the books to the library." She didn't answer any more of his emails or visit him.

Now, she faced a new challenge. Her dad was dead and Uncle Dan was like a vulture swooping in for roadkill. She was the roadkill. He claimed that he wanted to help her run the bookstore. But she had only seen a few times over the years because of his endless string of global adventures. He was a stranger.

A doomsday scenario stabbed Meg's heart. She knew the store was failing and felt certain Dan would take off. After Dan's departure, Mark would break up with her, and she would have to beg for a low-level job at the public library. The job offer she turned down—to be the second in command of the county library system—was history. The position had been filled. Meg would be persona non grata. Her life would be over. Just before going off a mental cliff, her thoughts returned to the voicemail warning left on the office phone.

Assuming the caller was referring to *The Birds of America*, why leave it on Dad's machine? Who was the target? Could Dad be the deal maker? Or uncle Dan? She thought Dad was an honest man, working with Portland Police on several rare book thefts over the years. Still, that was before he got sick and before the bookstore's survival was in doubt.

Bruce had told Meg he was worried about her future. She tried to assure him that he would be around long enough to see her married, have kids, and give him grandkids. It was a lie. Bruce's health was rapidly deteriorating. Marriage might be near, but kids? Years away, if ever. Grandkids weren't possible during Bruce's shortened life. Although Stanfield would not say if her father was involved, she half suspected it. Dad had offered a clue when he said he was 'working on a plan to secure her future.'

Right now, she wasn't sure she had much of a future. Her eye was pulsing with pain, and her head pounding.

"Meg, are you okay?" asked Jansen, who was waiting for an answer to her question about possible suspects.

"I have no idea who the target was," said Meg, her mind roiling with the sordid details of her affair and Stanfield admitting the theft.

"Is it possible you were the target?"

"Oh my god. You think someone wants to kill me?"

"Meg, I know you're under a lot of stress. I'm sorry to have to question you. But there's a shooter out there. We need to track them down before someone else gets hurt."

Meg sank back onto the pillow and sobbed. "I was a librarian with a promising career. Now, I'm a spinster who sells bags of used books. I had little to offer before this mess. With only one eye, I have even less. Maybe I'd be better off dead."

"When did you become a drama queen?" Jansen snapped. "The Meg I know is a spunky, persistent, never-give-in and never-give-up woman. She sky dives, rock climbs and parasails. The Meg I know even hiked 500 miles of the Pacific Crest Trail—alone."

Meg sat up tall. "You're right, Kim. I need to quit being a weenie. I don't know what's wrong with me." Meg started biting her fingernails.

"Stop that," Jansen ordered.

"Sorry," said Meg.

CHAPTER 16

Jed

1

Jed stood at the stove preparing chorizo and eggs, Lexi's favorite. She craved Latin food. Plantains and beans, ceviche, arepas, chilaquiles, huevos ranchero, and plain old street tacos. You name it; she loved the flair, spiciness, and simplicity.

"That smells so damn good," said Lexi, standing at the kitchen door. "It reminds me of mornings with Mom and Dad exploring Mayan ruins. Our guides would cook up simple but spicy food, bursting with flavor. I couldn't get enough." She yawned.

"I guess you were up late painting the Orange-Bellied Parrot for Bill." He handed her a glass of papaya juice. She closed her eyes and sipped it.

"I know it was my idea to paint each rare bird we acquire. Unfortunately, each failed portrait reinforces my fear that I'm a lousy bird painter. I know we claim the Foundation is about saving disappearing species of rare birds, but I wonder if we're doing the right thing. I saw one estimate that only 14 of the Australian parrots live in the wild, with another few hundred in captivity. And they only live for two years. Aren't we catering to the whims of the wealthy?"

"Like us?" asked Jed. "Yeah, we're a selfish group of birding fanatics who get what they want. We're targeting birds not long for this world. But, if nothing else, the paintings capture them for future generations. I agree it may not justify capturing them for our members' personal gratification."

"Freezing them so scientists could clone them in the future would be better than stuffing them for display after they die," she said. "Do you think we could convince The Red Flock to invest in a cryogenic unit to preserve them?"

"We'll ask them," said Jed. "If we expanded our mission to preserve their bodies, would you feel better about capturing and painting them?" Lexi shrugged. "I'd feel better if I could make them come alive on canvas." Jed knew there was no quit in Lexi. Despite her increasing discontent with her bird paintings, she would keep painting until her birds leaped off the page—or die trying. She was relentless.

Lexi's mother was her role model for toughness, wading with Lexi's father through swamps and jungle while hiking to remote places to study indigenous cultures. Lexi was by her side, undeterred by bugs, snakes, heat, or tropical downpours. Back home, her dad took her hunting in the winter. He taught her to shoot and field-dress deer. In college, she learned to taxidermy pheasants, then draw them.

She earned top grades in high school and college for her animal illustrations, but average marks for wildlife paintings. "Too angular, dead looking," an art teacher told her. He pointed to the works of 19th Century painter Rosa Bonheur as an example of how to animate wildlife. "You can't merely stand back and observe," he told her. "You need to get bloody, like Bonheur, who attended livestock fairs, visited slaughterhouses, and dissected carcasses she bought from her butcher." And, of course, the professor touted Audubon's work. "The birds in his paintings fly, dive, and swim in vivid animation among flowers, trees, and landscapes," he said. "It's a talent you have to develop."

Jed walked over and put his arm around Lexi. "Let's talk about your paintings."

"Is this going to be tough love? Are you going to tell me to quit?"

"I want to give you some perspective and motivation for continuing your work. I've been researching Audubon's work and found some surprising information. Audubon and his assistants, figuratively speaking, left a trail of bloody feathers while getting enough specimens for him to paint. He needed them fresh before their colors faded so they appeared alive. Then he would stick wires inside to arrange them in lifelike poses. He had no deadlines; his paper and color palette were from natural sources. So, he had lots of advantages."

"How do I make up for my lack of talent?"

"You have extraordinary talent. You need to develop it. Keep it up. You'll get there. I think you could do it without paying an exorbitant amount for *The Birds of America*. We've both become obsessed with those paintings. I'm having second thoughts about owning a copy. Do we really need them? Legally and financially, they spell trouble."

Lexi disagreed, but she said nothing.

"Because you struggled with bird paintings, I dug deeper into Audubon's life and work and came up with this article."

Lexi read the headline, *Life and Death in Bird Art* by Don Luce, from a 2014 issue of the *Minnesota Conservation Volunteer.*

"Read the section I highlighted."

When she finished, she turned to him excitedly. "Jed, you can't believe how much better I feel. The words make me more determined than ever to be a great bird painter." She hugged and kissed him.

"You're turning me on, Cherry," he said. "Should we celebrate?"

"Later," she said. "I promise."

He smiled and caressed her cheek, then said, "Let me read it aloud for emphasis."

From an early age, John James Audubon was passionate about studying birds. He watched, collected, and drew them. But he was disappointed his drawings did not capture the sense of life and action observed in nature. He burned his failed efforts each year and started anew on his birthday. His father encouraged his interest in birds but told young Audubon it was impossible to capture nature's living essence in a drawing. Undeterred, Audubon continued his quest.

According to another part of the article, it took years and many failures to learn the painting technique he used. Lexi drank in the words like they were the Fountain of Youth.

... In his quest, he tried many tactics. He strung up freshly killed birds with thread and drew them. The few surviving examples of these drawings show the results were unsuccessful. He then decided to make drawings in the field as he watched birds. Because birds, of course,

move, he could capture only sketchy outlines. But this practice trained him to observe and remember the characteristic postures and manners of each species.

His bird drawings slowly became more lifelike. Finally, he hit upon a method. Remembering the actions of the bird, he would pin and wire a newly shot bird to a board in a natural pose. The board was marked off in a grid. Using the same grid marks on his paper, he could outline the bird in the correct proportion.

With this technical challenge solved, Audubon was freed to paint birds the way he loved, alive and moving in nature. He created dramatic compositions in which life-size birds fly, dive, and swim in vivid animation among flowers, trees, and landscapes. He gave the viewer a window into the lives of his beloved birds. Birds were no longer mere specimens to be cataloged. They were beings leading interesting and intrinsically valuable lives. This was a revolutionary breakthrough, which ultimately resulted in Birds of America, his collection of 435 prints.

"Jed, let's celebrate," she said, grabbing his hand. The articles had given her new energy. "Let's do masks and all."

She reached down, playfully brushing the front of his jeans. "I think you're ready," she said, smiling. "Forget the masks."

2

"I've got to get back to my studio and finish the parrot painting," said Lexi, in the afterglow of one of their more vigorous love-making sessions. "A few touches more, and I'll have a picture I can live with."

"Are we set for tonight's Tenth Gathering of The Red Flock?" Jed asked, reading from the invitation she had sent. It would be the tenth delivery of an endangered bird species to a member who had requested—and paid dearly for one.

In each case, the poaching network, disguised as a bird preservation group, acquired the desired species and delivered the bird to Jed. The requesting member would come to the tropical aviary the C-14 Foundation built on the Miller estate. The member would have time with the bird; they would hold hand-feed it. One of C-14's members had been a professional photographer. She would come over and take candid shots of the bird with the member and then present them later with a stunning portrait. Finally, Lexi would showcase the bird's painting at a Red Flock party, then hang it in The Red Flock Avian Gallery, located in the Miller home.

Jed handed Lexi another glass of papaya juice.

"We're ready," she said, then focused on her drink. "This papaya is like breathing fresh tropical air. I feel like I'm on a beach in Brazil."

"The RSVPs are in, and everyone is coming, including Colin Byrne. The food is being prepped. The wine is in our cellar."

"Great job," said Jed.

"Did you brief Dr. Briggs?" Lexi asked.

"Yes, he knows exactly how the ceremonies are performed and his role. Let's go over the schedule for the evening's activities."

"We'll assemble in the aviary for rum punch and Brazilian hors d'oeuvres," said Lexi. "At 7 pm, the Flock will move to the gallery, where the ceremony will begin with Bill Masterson standing in the center of the room. Once we complete the parrot painting presentation, we'll move to the dining hall for a roasted pheasant dinner with finger potatoes and a kale salad with squab-infused dressing. We'll have four courses with Byrne Vineyards wines matched to each course."

"I'll be emcee, as usual," Jed said. "I'll introduce Briggs, describe options for our next group birding trip, give a short financial overview of C-14, and announce our next requested acquisitions, numbers eleven through fourteen."

"Do you think Briggs is up to it? Can we count on him?" Lexi asked.

"I think he's solid and motivated. He wants to get out of the dog care business and into avian medicine. So, we're giving him a big boost. Besides the annual pay and signing bonus, he'll make a bundle from our members requesting extra services."

"Looks like we're ready," said Jed.

Lexi nodded, kissed Jed, and headed to her studio to finish her parrot painting. Jed headed to his own wing for a shower where he could listen to the news on speakers installed in the bathroom walls. He tuned into KOIN in time for an alert.

"Breaking news ... The body of Marc Stanfield, 42, former curator of the rare book room at the Portland Central Library, was found today inside a safe in the basement of McQuillan's Bookstore. Police are saying little else about the bizarre discovery. We have a reporter on the way to the scene. Stanfield is the man accused of stealing the library's copy of The Birds of America, books worth millions, before he disappeared. Stay tuned for more details as they become available."

Had Lexi killed Stanfield to get her hands on *bird books*? No way. But she did rave about her visits to the library to see the Audubon paintings and Stanfield. Jed never gave it much thought in the past. The visits were often late and lasted for hours. Was there something more going on? Were they lovers? Jed's mind was racing down a black hole. Finally, he snapped himself back to reality. But hadn't she said more than once she would kill for a copy? Wasn't she merely expressing her intense desire for the books. He pushed his thoughts away.

CHAPTER 17

Meg

1

A knock on her hospital room door made Meg's head snap up. Who now? Couldn't the nurses leave her alone?

"Are you decent?"

"I'm decently ugly. You can enter if you can bear to look at your one-eyed girlfriend."

"You mean fianceé," said Mark Larson.

"I'm damaged goods. Chances are I'm going to be a one-eyed freak—a cyclops." She couldn't help evoking the image of the beast from *The Cyclops*, a 1957 movie she often watched with her Dad. It had scared the hell out of her.

"I liked that movie, too," said Mark. "It was required watching as part of a college course on Greek and Roman themes in literature. I'll close one eye, pretend I'm a cyclops, and see what I see."

"Gaze upon me at your own risk."

"I see a beautiful woman who is slightly battered. I like the bandage. Worse case, you get a patch and can claim to be a pirette." Meg cocked her head.

"A female pirate. You could wear different color patches the same way you change colors on your toenails. You could match the nails and patch. Make a fashion statement." Meg smiled.

"Look through that one eye at me and tell me what you see," he said.

"I see a handsome, sexy blonde man with a crewcut, big shoulders, nice glutes, and a winning smile."

79

"Perfect. We see eye to eye, each with one eye closed. You're beautiful. I'm handsome. Maybe I'll poke my eye out, and we'll have one good pair."

Meg giggled. "You'd better not. I love those blue eyes. Both of them."

Just then, an aide arrived with a wheelchair.

"Are you ready to go home?" she asked.

"Can't wait," she said, plopping into the chair for the trip to the curb. Finally outside, she was able to breathe in the fresh Northwest air for the first time in a week. A burst of energy and optimism filled her. A moment later, Larson pulled up and helped her into the car.

When they arrived at Meg's apartment, Mark helped her to the elevator, then waited for her to find her keys to the front door.

"Give me a kiss, pirate girl."

"Not funny." She kissed him anyway. "But don't bother to come in with me and don't worry about me. I'll be fine. I need some time settling back into my routine at home, alone."

After she closed the door, Meg took one look at her home, fell on the couch, and cried.

2

Her dingy one-bedroom apartment—all she could afford on savings left over from her librarian job—was the same lonely place she left a week before. She had to get out of there. But, first, she needed to eat. The hospital food was better than she thought it would be. Still, it was not what she liked.

She pulled a coconut-flavored Icelandic yogurt from the refrigerator, toasted a piece of bread, and spread a thick layer of peanut butter. She had this for breakfast nearly every morning and, like today, sometimes for lunch or dinner. After she finished eating, she grabbed her purse and headed across the street to the bus stop. She had to see McQuillan's. Or what was left of it. She had almost no memory of the shooting or the aftermath, so she wasn't sure what to expect.

She used the TriMet ticket app on her phone as she entered the bus. The driver surprised her when he asked what had happened to her eye. Before she could answer, the driver said, "I recognize you. You're Bruce McQuillan's daughter. I know your Dad. You were injured at his memorial."

"That's me." The driver's outburst made her cringe. She hated drawing attention to herself. Other riders who overheard the conversation offered condolences as she worked her way to a seat behind the back door.

"Here's the McQuillan stop," the driver shouted as if it had been named in Bruce's honor.

"Thanks," said Meg. She got off the bus and walked a block to the bookstore. Yellow tape blocked the entrance. She ducked under the tape and unlocked the door, ignoring the *Crime Scene, Do Not Enter* warning. Dried blood and broken glass covered the floor. She looked down and realized she had stepped on Dad. Or at least his ashes. "Sorry, Dad." Tears streaming down her cheeks, she rushed out of the building. She locked the door and headed home.

Stepping into the apartment, loneliness enveloped her like a wet blanket. Her breath felt labored, the events of the past week pressing down on her. She had to escape. She pulled out her phone and called Mark, who picked up on the first ring.

"I want to come over to your place and spend the night."

"Give me an hour and I'll come pick you up," said Mark. "I have a mandatory meeting with the chief to brief him on the shooting, then I'll be right over."

"I'm lonely and miserable. And I'm horny. You're the only remedy."

"I'll take care of that," he said. "See you soon."

3

Meg and Mark went at each other like teenagers. She had to warn him to be careful of her eye and the stitches.

Afterward they had dinner, watched TV, and returned to bed. They plunged into another round of lovemaking before falling asleep. The following day, they woke up early and drove to Ovation Cafe at The Field Park, where they had coconut scones and Moroccan lattes for breakfast. Afterward, Mark dropped Meg home before heading to the police bureau.

After he left, Meg began the mile walk to the lawyer's office for the reading of Bruce's will. The air was crisp with blue skies, a lovely day even with one eye.

She stopped to pull in the smell of pine trees from nearby Forest Park, then zipped her jacket and pulled the hood over her hair.

Thirty minutes later, she entered the offices of Egan and Egan, Attorneys at Law. Spencer Egan had been Bruce's attorney for 20 years. The second Egan on the door was Marion, Spencer's wife.

The office was decorated with large portraits of Portland urban scenes. Mrs. Spencer was a noted photographer with frequent showings of her work at local galleries. She claimed it was a hobby, but her obvious talent was beyond what you'd expect from someone snapping casual pictures for fun.

Uncle Dan was already there when Meg arrived, drinking an espresso and eating a muffin. He jumped up and hugged her. She gave him a quick pat on the back and pulled away. He had only been in their lives for four or five weeks. And just how long he would stay, she couldn't be sure. So much had happened since his arrival, it felt like forever. She realized she wasn't happy with him being there, despite his claim of good intentions to help her and Dad.

Meg's feelings were a mix of jealousy and distrust of the man. He had rarely come around when she was growing up. She never remembered him hugging her before today. He was a cool, detached man who had no children. Was helping Dad die a way to claim half of McQuillan's Bookstore? Now he was sitting with her, no doubt waiting to hear what his cut would be.

"Dan, from the little bit Dad has told me, you hated the family business and were a globe-trotting hobo on one endless adventure while Dad worked his fingers to the bone trying to keep McQuillan's alive. So why are you here?"

Dan looked at her. "Hobo is harsh. Bruce didn't feel that way."

"Hobo is *my* description of your life, not Dad's. Would vagabond be better?"

"Everything you say is true," said Dan. "But Bruce and I were close despite rarely seeing each other the past 30 years. We had a bond. I couldn't possibly blame him for what our Dad did, willing Bruce the entire store because I had other ambitions. To Bruce's credit, he never pressed me to come back. I loved him for that. Before he died, he said he wished he had followed in my footsteps. He said running McQuillan's had provided a comfortable living for many years but was dreary and lonely at times. Your presence during college summer vacations made him feel alive.

"I'll never forget something my brother told me years ago during one of my infrequent visits: *Life is a song - sing it. Life is a game - play it. Life is a challenge - meet it. Life is a dream - realize it. Life is a sacrifice - offer it. Life is love - enjoy it.* The quote is from Indian spiritual leader Sai Baba. Bruce was a dreamer and no doubt lived and experienced life's adventures through books."

Meg offered a half-smile, trying hard not to tear up. She decided not to dig further into Dan's motivations for being there. She didn't care about his ambitions other than leaving Portland and traveling. She didn't care where he went, as long as he left. Before they could talk more, Spencer Egan walked into the conference room.

"Sorry about the short notice for today's reading," said Egan. "Your Dad asked me to ensure all aspects of the business and finances were cleaned up and your future assured within 10 days of his death. I never asked why he set a deadline, nor did he explain. Dan, I can see you have something to drink. Meg, anything for you?" Meg shook her head.

"When was the will created?" asked Meg.

"Ten years ago, but he recently updated it. Let me read it. It's two pages. The bookstore represents most of the few assets he owned."

Half of nothing is nothing, Meg thought. While Dan was waving from the pier, she would drown in debt, a rat sinking with the ship.

"His will leaves McQuillan's Books and all its contents to both of you equally. In addition, Bruce asked me to read the following:

"If Spencer is reading this letter, then I have passed. Passed is such an odd term for death. Dan was unfairly cut out of his inheritance by our father because he chose not to work in the store. He deserves half of what father gave me. My half, of course, goes to Meg. With Dan's financial background and Meg's experience with books and sales, I hope the two of you have a fighting chance to save McQuillan's. If that's what you want.

"I told Dan and I will tell you, Meg, that I'm not the least vested in the bookstore's continuation unless it can help you make a living. It was a great idea our grandfather had back in the 1930s. The only flaw in his plan was to rent rather than buy the building. As a result, when I inherited the store, there wasn't enough money or credit to buy the property. There is nothing we can do about that. As you know, the book publishing and selling world has transformed, and I've failed to keep up. If you two can make a go of it, great. Otherwise, close

the store and find a new way to make a living. Go on an adventure. As a friend once said,
carpe diem, every damn day. Never look back."

"One more thing," said Egan. "Meg, here's a key to your Dad's safe deposit box. I have no idea what's in it. Whatever it holds is yours and yours alone. Here's a note that goes with it."

Meg pulled out the note. "A little something for your future. Love, Dad."

"You now have everything Bruce gave me. I wish you both the best. Of course, please call if I can do anything to help with this transition. Bruce was a client but also a dear friend. We shared our love for books. I often dropped in to see him and get his recommendation for best reads."

They thanked Egan and followed his secretary into the lobby. When they got to the street, Dan hugged Meg and whispered in her ear, "Do you want me to go to the bank with you?" His closeness made her skin crawl. She pulled away.

"Dad said it's for me." She pulled the note and key to her chest like a girl holding a doll to keep it away from her sister.

Dan held his hands in the air and backed away. "I just thought I might help."

"Uncle Dan, it's not like we've been close. On one of your rare visits, you helped Dad kill himself. Today, I find out Dad rewrote his will, and you get half the store. I appreciate your review of our records and advice you've given on tightening up finances. Still, I don't see us as business partners."

"I didn't want to be part of McQuillan's 30 years ago, and I still don't. So, anything I would do would be to help you get the store back on its feet."

"Nice thought. But it's dead, like Dad said. Its time has passed. I figure selling the store's inventory, including some rare books and magazines, might net $50,000. My half would be $25,000, enough to pay six months' rent while I job search."

"Meg, you can have my half."

"Why would you do that? Don't tell me it's out of love."

"Inheriting half the business for me was a victory alone. Our father treated me like crap after I said my dreams didn't include schlepping books and dusting bookshelves. Bruce bequest has given me the respect I wanted—the respect our father never would."

"Thanks for explaining," she said, a little embarrassed at her tirade.

"Unlike me, Meg, you love books and being around them. So why not find a new location, pull the best of McQuillan's inventory, and start fresh with a smaller, modern store with author talks, book readings, and group events? Create a cafe. Sell books, coffee, and pastries. It could be profitable." Meg looked at him, taking in his suggestion, trying to visualize a new beginning as a modern bookseller with an online presence and marketing to locals.

"Just think about it," said Dan when she didn't respond to his suggestion.

"I'm going to the bank and check out the safe deposit box," Meg told Dan.

"Need a ride?"

"Thanks, I'm walking everywhere after being cooped up in the hospital," she said.

"Watch where you walk," he warned. "With one eye, depth perception can be tricky. I had an injury once that left me with a patch for nearly three months."

She had forgotten the bandage over her eye. She reached up and smoothed the tape holding down the bandage. That would be just her luck: fall in the street and bash her head, leaving a dent and a big scar. A cyclops with a long row of stitches. At this rate, she would look like Frankenstein in no time. How would Mark feel about a girl who looked like she had been pieced together from other's discarded body parts?

4

Meg walked five blocks from the lawyer's office to a downtown Wells Fargo Bank branch. Like most big banks, large staffs had been replaced by ATMs and online services. Still, her Dad had maintained a box there for a decade. When she walked in the door, she saw a single teller. She explained why she was there and was directed to the room's far end. There, behind a cubicle wall, she found Morgan Williams. Her nameplate said she was a vice president.

"My dad just died and left me a key and the contents of a safe deposit box," said Meg, uncertain if the woman could help her.

"I'll need your name, identification, and account number to verify you're on the account," Williams said. Meg pulled out her driver's license and handed it to the woman. She studied the ID, trying to see past the bandage.

"I had an accident," Meg explained without being asked. Williams nodded and went to her computer, then a file drawer where she found the signature card.

"You're listed as co-owner," Williams said, showing her the signature card. Surprised, she nodded. She didn't remember signing any papers for a safe deposit box. Dad must have faked her signature to avoid getting her involved. He must have known she would have had to wait for weeks to get a death certificate to prove his death, then months more for the estate to settle, with little or no money to support herself or the store in the meantime.

The woman unlocked a drawer, pulled out a key ring, and told Meg to follow her. Inside the vault, the woman took Meg's key, inserted into the lock, along with bank's master key, and opened the door to the box. She pulled it out and handed it to Meg, straining from the weight. When Williams left the room, Meg opened it and found another note.

"For your future, whatever that brings. This $100,000 is a down payment from a deal I've made to sell a rare book. You'll get another $900,000 when the deal is complete. As I've said many times over my lifetime when you've asked me hard questions, *Ask me no questions and I'll tell you no lies.* Take the money. You deserve it. The real prize is in the safe in the bookstore's basement. You know the combination. You and Dan can discuss how to complete the sale."

Meg lifted a cloth under the note and saw stacks of $100 bills. Her one eye got big as she tried to take in the number of packets stacked 10 inches deep. When she recovered from the shock, she covered the money and called Morgan Williams, standing outside the room. After they relocked the box, Meg thanked Williams and headed out the door.

Meg knew she couldn't tell Dan. She feared he would claim half of the money, even though Dad's will was clear that the box's contents were hers, and hers alone. Did Dan know what was in the box? She couldn't take any chances. Then there was the question of Dad's deal. What kind of deal would have a $1 million payoff?

For a moment, *The Birds of America* flashed through her mind. Then she decided it wasn't possible. It would have required a secret deal between Marc Stanfield and her dad. Marc didn't know her dad, did he? Of course, he didn't. They'd kept her affair private, telling no one.

"Must be something else," she muttered. "Dad would never be involved with a theft from the public library. Anyone who tried to sell him a stolen book would end up in jail." Or would they?

Rather than go home, Meg needed to assess the damage at McQuillan's and reopen the bookstore. The landlord, sympathetic about the memorial shooting and Meg's injuries, said he would forgive a month's rent. Still, she needed to open the bookstore and begin generating sales or they would be out of business sooner than she imagined. She also wanted to see what Dad had put in the safe— the thing that would assure her future, the thing that would give her hope.

When she arrived at the store's front door, the crime scene tape had been removed. Inside, however, everything was the same. What was left of Dad was a million particles of ash covering everything near the bullet's point of impact. She would begin cleaning after she rescued Dad's gift from the safe.

She turned on the faint basement light and descended the creaky stairs. At the bottom, she stopped, let her eyes adjust in the dimness, then walked to the safe. "Here goes," she said, spinning the dial. She heard a click, then spun the safe handle. The locking rods retracted, and the door opened with a whoosh, dead air pushing out.

Stunned by smell, she stood back for a minute to allow the air to clear. It didn't. She stepped up, opened the door and looked in. Speechless at what she saw, her eyes got big, and she passed out.

CHAPTER 18

Mark Larson

1

"Jansen, you need to delay your vacation," said Larson. "I'm sorry."

"I want to go more than anything. What if I told you my mom is dying from cancer and has two weeks to live."

"You'll need a better excuse than that." Larson laughed.

"I already told Mom we would have to delay the visit for a few weeks," said Jansen. "But she's okay with it. I told her you loved cross-country skiing and shooting when you were a kid, and she suggested you come along."

Larson sat back in the chair with his eyes closed, drinking in memories of outdoor adventures in the endless snows of Sweden. "I'll think about it. Getting away for a week or two might be the best medicine for the bureaucratic paper-pushing blues."

"This case has more twists than a Hampshire Pig's tail," said Jansen. Larson's eye popped open, and he looked at her, waiting for more.

"I guess you want an update on the case?" she said as he stared at her.

"First, I want to know more about Hampshire pigs," he said. Mindless banter was the way Larson and Jansen dealt with stress. It calmed their minds.

"If you must know, they're found in England and Scotland, have erect ears, and naturally curly tails."

"Are they good to eat?"

"Their meat is very lean. At least that's what I read."

"Why are you reading stories about pigs? Never mind. Let's talk case details."

Before Jansen could begin, the duty sergeant at the front desk buzzed Larson.

"Chief, I thought you should know that two officers just responded to a 9-1-1 call at McQuillan's Books. Paramedics are on the way."

"Any more details, Sergeant?" Had the person who fired at the memorial returned to killed Meg? Would he have to identify her bloody body? Acid filled his throat as a wave of panic washed over him.

"Apparently, a digital watch alerted operators that someone had fallen and had not responded to the operator's attempt at contact. I'll be damned if I believed those watches worked as emergency beacons. Now we know."

"Thanks, Sergeant," said Larson. "We'll head to the scene."

Larson tried to dial Meg. It rang several times, then went to voicemail.

"Jansen, let's hit it. Emergency call at McQuillan's."

Larson got halfway down the hall and ducked into the men's room. Luckily, it was empty. He rushed into a stall and threw up. "Oh, no, not again," he said to no one. "I lost Helen. I can't lose Meg."

Jansen followed Larson into the men's room and listened. She heard his cries.

"Mark, we don't know if Meg is hurt. Rinse out your mouth, and let's hit the road." Larson followed her instructions and dried his face.

They ran to Larson's car and raced the mile between the Portland Police Bureau and McQuillan's with lights and sirens. When they pulled up front, they saw a fire department paramedic loading an empty stretcher into the back of the fire rescue truck. Were they too late? Was the stretcher empty because the victims were dead? Larson jumped out of the car and ran over to the paramedic. "How many victims?"

"A man and a woman," the paramedic said, looking bored and unconcerned.

Larson suddenly was wobbly, his knees about to buckle. Jansen saw him and jabbed his ribs with her elbow. It was enough to distract him, but his heart was pounding in his ears. "The woman is okay," the paramedic finally said. "She apparently fainted when she opened a safe downstairs and found a man's body inside."

"A body in a safe?" Jansen asked.

Larson and Jansen looked at each other with puzzled looks on their faces.

"The body has been there for a while," the paramedic said.

2

Larson and Jansen exhaled a massive breath of air simultaneously. Meg was still alive. "Thank God," said Larson. He was laughing and crying at the same time.

"Pull yourself together," said Jansen. "Let's find out what happened." Larson wiped his face on his coat sleeve.

Jansen rarely let her feelings loose. In her family, people just didn't cry. Besides, between Larson and Meg, she felt like she was caring for two crybabies; tears seemed to flow 24/7. Yes, they loved each other. But come on. They were wearing her out.

When Larson walked into the bookstore, Meg ran to him. "I'm so sorry," she said. "I should have told you about Marc."

Larson scooped her up in his arms and hugged her. "It's okay," he said.

Jansen interrupted. "Meg, tell us what's going on. Who's the victim? How do you know him?"

"It's Marc Stanfield."

"Who?" Larson asked.

"Stanfield is the guy who disappeared after the theft of the Central Library's copy of Audubon's *Birds of America*," said Jansen. "I pulled the cold case file and evidence box and read the details. The bound folios of Audubon's bird paintings from the early 19th century were stolen last year. With no sign of a break-in, the case notes say it appeared to be an inside job. The investigators theorized that Stanfield was the thief and sold them on the black market. After Stanfield disappeared without a trace, Alice Munson, who led the investigation, got pulled off to help deal with the Black Lives Matter protests, Antifa attacks, and downtown vandalism. Munson said they found no evidence of money flowing to Stanfield's bank accounts."

She turned to Meg and asked, "How do you know him?"

Meg took a deep breath and made her confession. She looked down at her feet and said, "I worked at the library with him. We started having lunch together. He began sharing stories about his financial and marital problems. Shortly after, we were in a relationship. Hell, I might as well be honest. We had an illicit love affair. It went on for several months until he disappeared. I heard nothing from him for six months. Then I get his recent text out of the blue."

She lifted her head to look directly into Larson's eyes and said, "I love you. Nothing happened. I didn't cheat on you. I went to see Marc, who had been hiding in Eastern Oregon under an assumed name. He had changed his looks, had grown a beard and ponytail, and was wearing overalls. He said he has been working as a ranch hand."

"Are you saying the man downstairs is Marc?"

"It's him."

"Wait here," Jansen said to Meg. "Larson, let's check it out."

They navigated the rickety staircase into the dank basement. In the far corner, partially hidden by rusty metal bookshelves, Coroner Lisa Begley was examining a body.

As they walked closer, the smell of rotting flesh hit them. Both pinched their nostrils to stifle the odor.

"How long has the victim been there?" Larson asked.

"A few days, maybe a week," said Begley. "My guess is that he suffocated." She lifted his hands to show bloody fingertips—a desperate attempt to claw his way out.

Larson recounted the case details to Begley. "First, someone used a high-powered rifle to blow up Bruce McQuillan's memorial. Then, the shooter leaves a voicemail demanding a mysterious bird book or else. Now Marc Stanfield turns up dead. What the hell is going on?"

Begley shook her head as she listened. "What you have is a helluva mess on your hands."

"You can say that again," said Larson.

Could Meg have locked Stanfield in the safe to scare him, angry over him dumping her, he wondered? Was this enough reason to kill someone in such a gruesome manner? He pushed the thought away.

"Jansen, let's go upstairs and talk to Meg," he said. "I'm sure there's more to the story."

Despite his fears over her possible guilt, Larson said, "Meg, would you be willing to ride to our office to help figure out how Marc Stanfield's death fits into our case?"

"Of course," she said. He hugged her and whispered in her ear, "I love you," then led her to his car.

3

After settling in a private conference room with coffee, Meg's confession poured out.

"Mark, I'm sorry I went to see him. Please believe me, nothing happened. I was still in shock that he was alive after months of grieving. At first, I thought he had another woman, then figured he was dead. Then he shows up without sending so much as a text for over six months. Finally, when I saw him, he said he was tired of hiding. He admitted stealing *The Birds of America*. He claimed he did it for his family and that our affair was a mistake. The books were going back to the library, he said. I agreed it was the right thing to do."

"Did he tell you if others were involved?" Jansen asked.

"He said there were 'accomplices' who wanted to complete the sale to an unidentified buyer. He claimed he didn't know the buyer and had pledged to never reveal who had arranged the sale."

"McQuillan's sells rare books," said Jansen. "I know Bruce has helped us with several rare book theft cases. Is there a chance he was involved?"

"I've thought about it but didn't want to believe it," said Meg. "Until yesterday afternoon."

"What happened yesterday that changed your mind?" Larson asked.

"After reading the will, I went to Dad's safe deposit box and found $100,000 cash. A note said the money was for my future and I could expect to receive another $900,000."

Jansen whistled at the amounts. "Did the note say where the money was from?"

"No," said Meg. "Just that the money would be wired to my checking account when the deal was done. I'll get the note for you, and you can read it."

"One more thing I just thought of," said Meg. "Uncle Dan was at the will reading this morning. He gets half the business. When the lawyer handed me the safe deposit key and note, he seemed eager to go to the bank with me. I told him thanks, but I would go alone."

Larson turned to Jansen. "Would you assemble the troops for a briefing? I need a few minutes with Meg."

"Will do, boss."

"This information changes nothing between you and me," Larson told Meg. "You and I are getting married. I'll quit the police department before I let you slip away."

"Do I have to give back the money?" said Meg. "I'll go broke if I do. It's a lifeline."

"Maybe not if it was legal. We don't know yet where it came from. Bruce might have been saving it for years. I'll cash in my pension if you need to give back the money. Then, we can run McQuillan's together."

"You would do that?" Meg's face lit up. He nodded and smiled.

"I would never let you invest in McQuillan's, but I might welcome an investor in a new store. Would you want to sell books after the excitement of being a cop?"

"I might be good at selling books," he said. "I can tell you I'm not much good at paperwork and managing detectives. They're like herding cats. Now, let's get you out of here. I'll have a patrol car run you home."

"No, I'll walk. The sun is shining, and the birds are chirping. It feels good to be alive."

"One more thing," said Larson. "Any idea where Stanfield hid *The Birds of America*?"

"He didn't say where, only that they were securely locked away."

In the safe? Larson wondered.

CHAPTER 19

Jansen

1

"I need a beer," said Jansen.

"Me, too," said Larson. "After our team meeting, we can go to The Library."

The Library Taphouse and Kitchen was a four-minute walk from the police bureau. The servers introduced themselves as *librarians* to help you choose from a collection of 100 beers on tap. The pub was a local favorite.

"We're running in place," said Jansen. "We close the cold case on who stole the books but open a murder investigation. And we still have no idea who has the books. Or who and why someone fired a high-powered rifle at the memorial." Greed was no doubt a factor in the murder. Why else would anyone kill for a book with bird paintings?

"I like birds," said Larson. "I went birding with my parents when I was a kid in Sweden. Still, what's so special about Audubon?" He looked at Jansen, waiting for an answer.

"I had the same question, and now I know the answer. Are you ready to be dazzled by my brilliance?" Larson rolled his eyes.

"Here goes. There is this amazing service called Google. Good old Google will find an answer if you have a question—no matter how dumb."

"Hilarious," said Larson, shaking his head. "Go on, dazzle me."

"Audubon was a noted ornithologist—a bird expert. *The Birds of America* is a book, but it's not."

"You're not making sense," said Larson. "What is it?"

"*The Birds of America* is four books. They include 435 hand-painted drawings of 700 bird species Audubon created between 1827 and 1838."

"Enough of the history lesson," said Larson. "Bottom line, a set is worth a couple of million?"

"How about $12 million?" she fired back. "Shouldn't you know the value? You were the hot-shot security consultant at Paragon Systems in charge of protecting the library's rare book room."

"You know the answer to that. Yes, I was at Paragon last year. I took over *after* the Audubon theft. I love books, so I can't tell you why I never focused on what was in the rare book collection. Too busy running Paragon's entire northwest region, I guess." Larson and Jansen agreed that whoever locked Stanfield in the safe had likely stolen the four volumes, assuming they had been hidden there.

"Let's go over the suspect list," said Larson.

"First, there's Meg McQuillan," said Jansen. Larson cringed. But he didn't protest.

"She gave up her library dream job to become the CEO of McQuillan's Books, a failing business. She had an affair with Marc, who she thought had blown her off for another woman. Then he popped up, ready to return *The Birds of America* to the library, killing the deal to sell them and her inheritance. Then he's found dead in the safe. The next suspect is Bruce McQuillan. Based on the note in the safe deposit box, he was doing a deal to give Meg a million dollars for her future," Larson added. "Bruce may have killed Stanfield to prevent him from backing out of the sale. The timeline between Bruce's death and when Stanfield was killed is tight. We'll have to wait for the coroner to give us a more accurate time of death for Stanfield. Is it possible Bruce figured he would die and had nothing to lose? He wanted to ensure a legacy for Meg. But why would Stanfield agree to get in the safe?"

"When I came over here to look at the crime scene," said Jansen, "the CSI showed me a gun in a drawer under the cash register. I checked it out and found that it was purchased long ago and registered properly. Bruce must have kept it for protection. A threat to shoot Stanfield might have convinced him to get in the safe. Still, what a way to go. I would prefer getting shot."

"Maybe he intended to scare Stanfield, letting him out after a while," said Larson. "Then decided he couldn't take a chance Stanfield wouldn't change his mind. Lots of possibilities and little evidence. Let's bring the troops up to speed and have them help get some answers."

"One more possibility," said Jansen. "The wife, Ginny Stanfield, was having financial and marital problems, according to Meg. And she may have been pissed her husband was cheating on her."

"Add Mrs. Stanfield to our growing suspect list," said Larson. "If she's the killer, we'd have to figure out how she lured him into the safe."

2

Jansen called a meeting in the squad room to update the other detectives.

"Nothing is easy," said Jansen to the assembled group. They looked at her, waiting for more.

"We have new developments in our case—or should I say cases. The body of Marc Stanfield turned up today in a safe in the basement of McQuillan's Books. The coroner says he suffocated, and his bloody fingers show he fought desperately to get out."

"That's crazy shit," said Detective Munson. "Right out of Edgar Allen Poe."

"There's more. Because Meg McQuillan admits to having an affair with Stanfield, she's a suspect. Munson, the Stanfield theft and his disappearance was your case originally; you must have met Ginny Stanfield, the victim's wife."

"As I recall, I asked a few questions about her relationship with her husband, whether she thought he stole the books, and where he might have gone. She claimed to have no knowledge of what her husband might or might not have done. I believe she was mystified at his disappearance and feared he was dead. She insisted her husband would never steal from the library. She started crying."

"Take another run at her," said Jansen. "See if you can get a court order to look at her bank records. Let's see if she's received any large cash deposits."

Jansen agreed to investigate Meg McQuillan when none of the other detectives volunteered. She couldn't blame them. Who would want the job of drilling down on the Chief Detective's fianceé.

"I'm also going to talk to Colin Byrne," said Jansen. "He a winemaker but also a birder and the former chair of the Portland Audubon Society—someone well connected in local birding circles. So, he might have ideas about who would want *The Birds of America* enough to kill for it."

Jansen directed Det. Mandy Millbrook to check out Dan McQuillan's background. He just inherited half of McQuillan's Books. Given the value of the books, even a discounted sale would leave millions for him and other conspirators to split.

Jansen asked Detective Sal Berenson to meet with Bill Bowman, curator of the rare book room at the library. "Find out if he has any theories about the case or suspects. Bowman is a sharp guy with an encyclopedic memory and handwritten visitor logs, as backup. He knows who comes to see the library's rare books and why. He helped solve the Colin Byrne case last year."

Larson, who had remained quiet through Jansen's briefing, then stepped up. "I know what you're thinking. Go easy on the chief's girlfriend. That's bullshit. Do your jobs. Go where the evidence takes you. We're cops first. Yes, Meg McQuillan is my fianceé, but at this point, she is also a suspect, as much as it pains me to say it. So let's attack this case."

"You got it, Chief," detectives Munson, Berenson, Millbrook, and Jansen responded in unison as if rehearsed.

"Larson, guess we'll have to pass on the beer," said Jansen. "I need to call Colin Byrne and run a hunch by him, get his thoughts on the case."

"While you guys are trying to get your arms around this elephant, I'm going to spend some time with Meg," said Larson.

"I know your champing at the bit to question Meg after she admitted having an affair with Marc Stanfield. That's all in the past. Put it in a box. Move on. Otherwise, you'll screw up your relationship with Meg and cross a huge ethical line."

"Yes, ma'am," said Larson.

"Just looking out for you," she said.

Jansen returned to her desk and called Colin Byrne.

CHAPTER 20

Jansen

1

Colin Byrne picked up on the first ring. "Detective Jansen, how the hell are you?"

"Doing well. How are you settling in?"

"Feeling free as a bird. A thrilling sensation."

"You've done your time and paid for restoring the blood-stained copy of The North American Indian," said Jansen. "Everyone was pleased with the outcome of the case. Now, I need your help on a new case."

"Should I be worried? Am I a suspect?"

"No, not at all. I need to tap your birding expertise. By the way, the 'Free as a Bird' theme for your homecoming party was very cute."

"Glad you liked it. Sorry, you couldn't make it. The shooting at McQuillan's no doubt took priority over drinking wine with an old jailbird."

Jansen cracked up. "That's too funny. And yes, the high-powered rifle shot that exploded Bruce McQuillan's cremation urn put a tiny crimp in our social life. What's your work status?"

"I'm back at it full-time—with some time off to fulfill my parole conditions. I'm giving regular talks to families about intergenerational violence," said Colin. "I find it a very healing practice for me. Hopefully, my experience helps others."

"How's the professor?" she said, referring to Colin's son, Bryan, a college professor in Arizona. Bryan had taken the reins of Byrne Vineyard Estate as CEO when Colin was in jail. "He's heading back to the classroom his wife and daughter."

"You're a grandfather?"

"It's a long story. I'll tell you over a glass of wine when you and Jim come for a visit."

"Anyone in *your* life?" Jansen asked.

"I've reconnected with a widowed girlfriend from college, and we plan to go on endless adventures when Bryan takes over in a couple of years. What adventures, I don't know. Some will include birding. Annie and I will figure it out together."

"I'm happy for you. Speaking of birds, my case is like the proverbial bird's nest under construction: full of bits and pieces with little shape. And I'm the mama bird who hasn't figured out how to put it all together."

Colin laughed. "Well, I'm not sure how good I would be at nest building either."

"We've got a murder, theft, and attempted killing that may or may not be related. Or they may all be linked with birding and bird books connecting them," said Jansen.

"How can I help?"

2

Jansen filled Byrne in on the intertwined incidents. He already knew about the shooting at McQuillan's and recalled the details of *The Birds of America* theft. However, Meg's confession and discovery of Stanfield's body were new.

"Do you know anyone who would want a copy of Audubon's book, and have the means to pay for it?"

"Lots of people. 1 would love to have a copy. Rich bird-lovers, rare book collectors, artists, naturalists, wildlife biologists. The list is endless. Jed and Lexi Miller are two fellow birders and friends who are desperate to own a copy. Jed just bid more than $11 million to buy a copy at an auction and lost out to a bidder who went to $12 million." Jansen made a note.

"I recently met Lexi at Andy's Firing Pen. She was practicing with a $50,000 elephant gun she uses to hunt big game."

"That's Lexi. A redhead whose hair is always on fire with some project, event, or cause. She's an expert pistol shooter with lots of gold medals, including for mixed events with men and women. At some point, she graduated from target shooting to big game trophy hunting."

Colin painted a less than flattering picture of Jed, a heart surgeon. "Like most multi-millionaires, Jed is constantly searching for the next big adrenalin rush—as if heart surgery isn't enough. Before my wife died, we joined the Millers and their friends on exclusive, rare bird-watching expeditions in remote parts of the world. We once cruised the Nile, stepping onto land near pods of the biggest damn crocodiles you've ever seen, to glimpse the Social Lapwing, a critically endangered species. It was crazy. And scary, even with guides armed with high-powered rifles to fend off the crocs."

"I still don't get the excitement," said Jansen. "How do you get turned on seeing a rare bird?"

"It's all in the chase—seeing, recording, and photographing a species that few in the elite birding ranks have ever laid their eyes on."

"Jed wanted to set the world record for spotting and recording by sight or sound the most bird species in one year. He fell short. His dad died, and he needed to go home to arrange the funeral. The partners in his medical practice also threatened to kick him out if he didn't return and help with the caseload. I know, it still doesn't compute for you, does it?"

"Nope."

"Do you like sports?"

"I like the superstars and their efforts to break records," she said.

"Jed Miller is like Tiger Woods attempting to break Sam Snead's record for all-time PGA Tour wins. He and Snead are tied with 81 wins each. Tiger doesn't want to be tied. He thinks he still has a shot at the record despite nearly losing a leg and numerous back and knee surgeries. The chase of the record motivates people like Tiger and Jed."

"Now, I follow you. Jed and Lexi are overachievers."

"Exactly. They never quit anything they start and never give in when faced with challenges. Now you understand their mindset. They are the triathletes and ultramarathoners of the birding world. Faster, higher, more is their mantra."

"What's their motivation for getting the Audubon books?"

"Prestige for Jed, putting him on top of the list of elite birders—an eagle among hawks."

"What's in it for Lexi?"

"Lexi is trying to figure out Audubon's technique for making his birds appear to be 3D so she can create an updated, technologically-advanced book. Think of it as *The Birds of America* on Steroids."

"How do you know so much about them?"

"I've spent hundreds of hours with them on bird-watching trips, drinking with Jed, and discussing our lives, hopes, dreams, and failures. Usually over a bottle or two of wine. Wine helps open the kimono."

"Hadn't heard that one before," said Jansen, suddenly laughing so hard the coke she was drinking squirted out of her nose.

"You're disgusting," said Munson, listening to Jansen's end of the conversation.

Jansen flipped her off and went on with her conversation.

"Sorry, Colin. That was hilarious. Still, I don't think you have enough material for a comedy career."

He laughed.

When she could talk without laughing, she asked, "Would they kill for a copy of *Birds*?"

"A loaded question," he said. "I doubt Jed would. Lexi is unpredictable. She can be incredibly intense in conversations about issues important to her or when practicing at the firing range. You feel she would like to kill someone or something when she gets focused and starts firing."

"Since you know them so well, you've probably heard Jim has taken a job as the C-14 Foundation's new veterinarian?"

"I have," said Colin. "I've just accepted the Foundation's offer to join. Their membership is limited to 14 members. One died, and I'm the person they invited to fill the slot."

Jansen, of course, didn't mention Jim's role as an FBI informant. Was Colin involved in the poaching scheme, about to face a long stretch in federal prison? Or was he the informant Agent Perez mentioned?

3

It was nearly 5 o'clock when Jansen walked into Larson's office, just as he was leaving to pick up Meg.

"Can we do this tomorrow?" Larson asked, his face pleading with her to let him go.

"Just give me minute."

He plopped back down in his chair and listened as she gave him a brief account of her conversation with Colin Byrne.

"The bottom line is that Lexi Miller has risen to the top of our suspect list. She is a skilled hunter with a big-game rifle. She is reportedly desperate to get her hands on a copy of *The Birds of America*. How Stanfield's theft and his death fit into this picture, or if he was working alone, is anyone's guess."

"An inch at a time," said Larson. "Listen, I've got to go. Meg is expecting me."

"You're going to get laid, aren't you? That's why you want to get out here." Larson face flushed.

"Go for it, Larson. I'll handle the end-of-day briefing."

After Larson left, Jansen called everyone into the incident room and began the update.

"Chief Larson has a meeting to attend, so I'm conducting our meeting."

Alice Munson held up a finger like she was too weak to raise her arm or didn't want to appear to be that overanxious first grader eager to please the teacher.

"Something weird is going on with the Stanfields," Munson said. "I went to their last known address. I walked around outside the house and looked in the windows. It was empty. No furniture, nothing. I knocked on neighbors' doors. They haven't seen the family in about a week.

"Do the neighbors have any idea why they left or where they went?" asked Jansen.

"Neither Mrs. Stanfield nor her daughter told anyone they were leaving," said Munson. "Not even an elderly lady who said that Ginny Stanfield came by daily to help her with chores. Her name is Etta Thompson. Mrs. Thompson, who lives across the street from the Stanfields, says Mrs. Stanfield was a saint. She started crying the more she talked about how much she loved the family. I asked her if she saw anything unusual going on at the Stanfield home. At first, she shook her head, then admitted that she's a night owl."

Munson looked at her notes and continued, "Mrs. Thompson said she witnessed men and women in dark suits hurry Ginny and her daughter into big black cars just after midnight. She didn't member which day. She said they drove away and never returned. She's made numerous calls to Mrs. Stanfield and has gotten no response."

"Damn FBI," Jansen mumbled.

Munson and the other detectives looked at her, waiting for more.

"It's nothing specific. I just know if little men in suits show up in black cars late at night, the FBI is usually involved. So, I'll call my contact there and see what I can find out."

CHAPTER 21

Jim

1

Jim Briggs walked out of the bedroom and into the den where Jansen was drinking a cup of tea.

Jansen looked up, scanned Briggs from head to toe, and spit up her tea. Standing before her was a six-foot-six towering red creature with a mask shaped into a red feathered face and a long yellow beak.

Jansen started laughing hysterically. Between gulps of breath, chortles, and rolling on the floor, Jansen said, "You look like a red version of Big Bird. You're kidding me, right? The Red Flock must be pulling a joke."

"No joke. This is standard attire for the ceremony tonight. I look ridiculous."

"That's an understatement."

"Everyone wears an outfit representing a red bird with a matching mask for the ceremony. Lexi designed this one, which is supposed to be ..."

"Big Bird," said Jansen, finishing his words with another round of side-splitting laughter.

" ... A red American Flamingo," he said.

"You know how to turn on a girl, Briggs. How about every time you want sex, you suit up in this costume and start flapping your wings? That should get me in the mood."

A second later, they both were laughing hysterically. Thank God the neighbors couldn't hear them through the adjoining soundproof walls of their townhouse. When they stopped laughing, they blew their noses and wiped away their tears. Finally, Jansen said, "I guess I better make sure you're wired up properly." She walked over, laughed again, then forced herself to stop as she checked the microphone placements. Briggs would wear them under black jeans, a black t-shirt, and a sports coat. The bird suit would go over the clothes. "Betty's agents know what they're doing," she said.

"I've got to get rolling," said Briggs, who had removed the bird suit and mask and packed them into a gym bag.

"Good luck, and remember that Lexi is a big game hunter, and you're the damn biggest game bird she'll ever see," said Jansen, falling into another laughing fit.

"Don't start," said Briggs, also cracking up.

"Good luck," she said, barely able to talk as she watched him leave.

2

From the smiles, hugs, and handshakes, Briggs could see the admiration the members of The Red Flock felt for one another and the rituals of the C-14 Foundation. As they stood in the Foundation's tropical aviary on the Miller Estate, sipping rum-spiced tropical punch, they pointed out their favorite birds darting around the room. They were like kids at the zoo.

"The bird sounds create a sweet symphony, don't you think?" Briggs overheard a Red Flock member say. Among the first to greet him was Bill Masterson, tonight's recipient of the Orange-Bellied Parrot.

"Dr. Briggs, welcome. How's my parrot?"

"He appears healthy," said Briggs. "A beautiful bird with a loud voice."

"I suspect you need a loud voice to be heard in a tropical forest," said Masterson.

"Good point."

Briggs felt a tap on his shoulder and turned around.

"Colin, how are you?" said Briggs.

"Free as a bird," said Colin.

Briggs laughed politely and said, "Sorry we missed your party. I'm sure Kim told you that police business kept us away."

"She did," said Colin. "You'll have to come out for a private tasting."

"We'd love that."

Colin turned to Masterson, shook his hand, and gave him a quick hug.

"Glad you're joining us," said Masterson. "I know you've waited a long time for an opening."

"I'm sure it will have been worth the wait," said Colin.

A moment later, Jed Miller appeared.

"I didn't know you knew Dr. Briggs," said Jed.

"His wife arrested me last year," said Colin. "And they like my wine. Except for the shooting at Bruce McQuillan's memorial, you would have seen them at my party."

"I know everyone is excited to have both of you as part of the Foundation."

Bill Masterson had drifted across the room to another group, and Jed excused himself when he heard his name called. Lexi was signaling that it was time to begin the parrot presentation ceremony.

"It's show time, friends. We'll meet in the gallery in 10 minutes."

3

Briggs stood alone in the middle of the Miller's avian art gallery, a towering red creature in a sea of tropical bird paintings. He was amazed at the palette of colors.

"You like what I've done?" The voice came from a masked person dressed as a Cherry-Throated Tanager.

"The murals of tropical scenes with birds in their native environment are stunning—the work of an artist talented in anatomy, color, and proportion," Briggs said.

"You're too kind."

"I mean it. It's truly inspired work. Adding the photos of the member's rare bird choices to the gallery also is inspirational."

"Again, you're very kind. What was not kind of me was to put a giant man in a flamingo costume." Lexi grabbed the sides of her head and laughed. "What have I done to you?"

"Between you and my wife, I've been a real barrel of laughs today."

When Lexi stopped laughing, she said, "Take it off—the costume. I didn't mean to humiliate you. I wasn't thinking about the wearer when I had it sewn."

"Done," said Briggs, who stripped it off and handed it to her. She took it and stuffed it behind a line of drapes in a corner.

"But keep the mask," said Lexi. I can explain to The Flock there wasn't time to complete your suit. We'll develop a more appropriate look for our next celebration."

A few minutes later, all 14 members of The Red Flock were assembled in a perfect circle around the table. From his position in the circle, Jed Miller stepped forward with a rifle.

Briggs went to the avian house where he retrieved the Orange-Bellied Parrot, then placed its cage on the table.

Bill Masterson walked into the circle, lifted the bird cage, and held it toward Jed as if making an offering or sacrifice.

Jed lifted the rifle, cocked it, and said, "My heart to your heart."

The others in the room responded, "Our hearts to your heart."

Jed fired the empty BB gun he used to kill the cardinal when he was 14.

After the shot, Jed lowered the gun, and the group said in unison: "Our hearts are one."

Jed briefly described the origin of the C-14 Foundation, a story they all knew well. It was like reciting The Four-Way Test at a Rotary meeting. The repetition reinforced the Millers' passion for the organization they had created.

When the story was finished, Jed said, "Saving birds is my passion and penance for what I did long ago." Everyone nodded their understanding.

Lexi stepped forward with the parrot painting she'd created for the gallery and showed it to everyone. They signaled their approval by slapping their sides with their elbows like they were doing the Chicken Dance.

After introducing Briggs and Byrne, Jed announced it was nearly time for dinner. He motioned for Lexi to come forward.

"Lexi, join me in the circle." He turned and picked up a cage and removed a red silk cover. Inside was one of the world's rarest birds, the Cherry-Throated Tanager—one of only 30 remaining.

"Your birthday present," said Jed. The group sang a round of happy birthday. Lexi put her hands over her heart as thanks, a line of tears on her cheek.

"This is the best present ever—perfect for a woman turning 50, who enjoys surrounding herself with pretty things, even as her beauty fades."

A series of cheers and well-wishes filled the room.

"Dinner begins in 15 minutes," said Jed.

Briggs left the room with the tanager and parrot. He videotaped the birds with his cell phone when he arrived back in the aviary. "An Orange-Bellied Parrot from Australia and a Cherry-Throated Tanager from Brazil are in these cages. They are part of a humanitarian program to save the species."

"What are you doing?" a voice from behind him said. "If I didn't know better, I would guess you would be giving a lecture to veterinarians."

He turned around and saw Lexi. "Exactly," he lied, quickly shifting from his undercover assignment to his role as Foundation veterinarian.

"I wanted to record this moment for the future. I can visualize teaching graduate classes at Oregon State's vet school. And I was thinking how I can use them to study bird behavior, so I can better care for them."

"A great idea," said Lexi. "But our non-disclosure agreement doesn't allow any documentation of our birds or operations. However, I'll recommend to the C-14 Board that we allow it. A contribution to the college could fund a lecture series."

"Lexi, that's a great idea. And, of course, I will keep all of this to myself, per the disclosure agreement. I'm crazy about birds and bird medicine. Working with the Foundation will be like earning a Ph.D. in tropical avian medicine. I'm holding two of the world's rarest bird species. Thanks to the Foundation, these and other species will be recorded and protected for all time. Perhaps we could eventually get a pair and set up a breeding program."

"Another great idea," Lexi added.

Briggs had worked out the explanation to allay any suspicion the Millers might have if he was spotted recording the birds. Apparently, the ploy satisfied Lexi.

She smiled. "Better hurry to the dining hall if you don't want to miss the hors d'oeuvres, especially the duck foie gras."

He hated foie gras; a gagging sensation pulled on the back of his throat. "Wouldn't miss it," said Briggs, faking a smile. "Give me a minute to get these guys settled."

She turned and walked away and left Briggs alone in the avian house. Briggs hit the send button on the videos, placed the birds in a protected area, and locked up as he left.

A few minutes later, Brigg's videos with his narration were in the hands of Betty Perez at the FBI office in Portland.

CHAPTER 22

Jansen

1

Detective Jansen walked a few blocks from the police bureau to the MAX Train stop and hopped on the Red Line toward Portland International Airport. The train was filled with the usual characters: the homeless, tourists, and locals heading to the airport for travel or work. A mishmash of urban dwellers. Thirty minutes later, she exited the train at the Cascade Station and completed her trip with a four-minute walk to the FBI's office.

Jansen loved the city's public transportation. Riding, rather than driving, was a way to slow down and give her time to think. Today, it gave her time to cool down. She was pissed off at Agent Betty Perez after discovering that the FBI had whisked away Ginny Stanfield, a potential witness in the Audubon case, in the middle of the night. Jansen added Mrs. Stanfield to her suspect list of likely killers. How could she not, given the woman's public humiliation after her husband disappeared, accused of stealing books worth millions?

Jansen entered the building, showed her ID to a security screener, and handed him her weapon to secure in a locked vault. Just as she completed screening, a woman approached her.

"I'm Agent Mary Ellen Beckworth," she said. "Here's your visitor ID. I'll take you upstairs for your meeting with Agent Perez." When they got off the elevator, Agent Beckworth, took Jansen to a conference room, offered her water, and said Perez would be along momentarily.

A few minutes later, Betty Perez walked in, all smiles, her arms extended as if to move in for a hug.

"I guess you're here to find out how Jim did on his first undercover operation?"

"Stop," said Jansen, her hand up, keeping Perez out of hugging range. "You've been holding out on me, putting your big FBI clodhoppers in the middle of my case."

"What are you talking about?" said Perez. "You agreed with the undercover operation."

"Yes, but I did not agree to your team hiding a potential key witness in one of my other cases."

"I have no idea what you're talking about."

"Don't bullshit me, Perez."

"Enlighten me," she shot back.

"One of my detectives went to the Stanfield home yesterday to interview Marc Stanfield's wife. The house is empty. An elderly neighbor said she saw men and women in dark suits with a big black car take Ginny Stanfield and her daughter away around midnight a week ago."

Perez took a breath, walked to the conference room's solid glass wall, and looked at the other agents buzzing around in the adjacent room.

"You know how we operate, Jansen. Need to know. We picked her up and moved her to a safe house. She's the star witness in the Audubon theft."

"She's a suspect in my case," said Jansen, too loud. Fortunately, the soundproof walls prevented her frustration from escaping the room.

Perez explained that *The Birds of America* is classified as artwork rather than literature, covered under U.S. and international laws established to protect major art and items of cultural interest.

"I've got a new twist for you, Betty," Jansen said, calming down. She realized federal laws would trump Oregon state statutes. "Ginny Stanfield is a suspect in her husband's murder."

Perez was now on her back foot. "Marc Stanfield is dead?"

"It was on the news last night. Where have you been?"

"Reading, drinking most of a bottle of wine, and avoiding the news."

"Meg McQuillan opened a safe in the basement of McQuillan's Books and found Stanfield's rotting corpse. The coroner estimates it had been there less than a week."

"Holy shit," said Perez.

"You can say that again," said Jansen.

"We saw Marc Stanfield and his accomplices as primary threats to her," said Perez. "Stanfield may be dead, but whoever conspired with him could be alive. Ginny told us that he was planning to give the books back, killing any deal that would have netted him and his associates millions. And would have given her a financial cushion for life. Potential risks to her life make protective custody the best option for her and her daughter."

"She fought the idea of moving to a safe house. I think she's being coy about her involvement. We hope she'll break down and tell us what she knows."

"I still have my own case to work under Oregon law," said Jansen. "Can we devise a plan to break this impasse and move forward?"

"I have an idea," said Perez. "Give me a minute. I need to make a phone call." Jansen watched Perez as she walked across the bureau work floor into her office and picked up the phone.

Jansen began pacing like a cat. The tightness in her neck was giving her a headache. She didn't want a battle over jurisdiction, especially with Betty. She certainly didn't want to jeopardize their friendship. Ten minutes later, Perez was back.

"I just called my boss. She's letting me decide whether or not to form a joint task force with the Portland Police Bureau to tackle my case and yours." Jansen's shoulders dropped, her body loosening. The tightness in her neck disappeared. She breathed a sigh of relief.

Jansen considered calling Larson first to get his okay but decided he would trust her to make the right decision. "Okay. We're in. On one condition: both sides share the information we gather. No holds barred. Mark Larson will need to bless the deal, but I'm confident he'll go along. I don't care who gets credit for what. I've got three open cases: the book theft, the memorial shooting, and Marc Stanfield's murder. It appears our cases are intertwined. I think a joint investigation will help both of us."

"Let's keep it small," Perez suggested. We can draw down additional resources as needed."

Jansen and Perez fist-bumped to seal the deal then Jansen opened her arms. "Give me a hug."

Perez looked out the conference room window to ensure they didn't have an audience, then hugged back.

"Betty, I suggest we use our place as a planning and meeting center. We're centrally located compared to your offices on the edge of the airport."

"Okay," said Perez. "When can we have our first meeting?"

"How about 3 p.m.?"

A few minutes later, Jansen was at the Cascade Station to catch the MAX Train back to her office. She called Larson to fill him in. "A great idea," said Larson. "I know you'll hold the FBI's feet to the fire so they share information."

"Count on it," she said.

Jansen hung up and texted Perez, "Larson is all in. See you at 3."

A thumbs-up text came in response.

2

With detectives and agents assembled for the afternoon strategic planning meeting, Jansen introduced Betty Perez and Agents Bobby Boyle, Melanie Acosta, and Jimmy Carlton, while Jansen introduced Alice Munson, Mandy Millbrook, Sal Berenson, and Larson.

Jansen walked over the Perez, leaned into her ear, and asked her if it was okay to talk about the poaching operation.

"Yep," said Perez. "Just don't reveal informant names or mention the ongoing undercover operation." Jansen nodded and stepped up to the front of the room.

"As all of you know, everything we discuss stays within this group. That means no pillow talk or discussing the case with your best friend over a beer. There is a lot on the line. We have four cases going simultaneously. First, Agent Perez will detail the FBI case, and then I'll tell you what our investigation has uncovered."

Perez stepped forward and outlined the anti-poaching case involving the C-14 Foundation, its founders, and the art theft case.

Jansen briefed the group on the memorial shooting and the Stanfield murder.

"*The Birds of America* theft case is interesting because recent developments in the past few days confirm that Marc Stanfield, who turned up dead this week in a safe at McQuillan's Books, is the thief. However, there are no clues about where the books are, whether he had one or more accomplices, or who bought or was planning to buy them. One key piece of evidence emerged following the discovery of his body. He apparently felt guilty about stealing the books from the public library where he was entrusted to care for them. He had planned to return them to the library and turn himself in."

"Detective Jansen, are you suggesting whoever killed Stanfield wanted to stop him from returning them?" Agent Boyle asked.

"That's our theory. Now we need to prove it."

Mark Larson stepped forward. "In the interest of transparency, I'm going to share some information we uncovered in the past 24 hours since Stanfield's body was discovered. The individual who discovered him was Meg McQuillan, daughter of bookstore owner Bruce McQuillan. She admitted having an affair with Stanfield before he disappeared." He explained that Stanfield came out of hiding to return the stolen books to the library.

Larson looked down at his shoes for a moment, then up at the group. "One more key piece of information: Meg McQuillan is my fianceé. I told my troops this at the beginning of our investigation—and I'm telling all of you: no one is above the law. You need to treat Meg McQuillan like any other witness or suspect. Follow the leads where they take you. Information about Meg McQuillan should be given to Agent Perez, not me. Let's keep this clean."

Larson's comment silenced the room.

"Thanks for your candor, Chief Detective Larson," said Perez.

"Are we clear on this issue?" Jansen said, making eye contact with each person in the room, getting their acknowledgment with a nod or a yes.

"One final note, then we need to get to work," said Perez. "Detective Jansen and I, who started as rookies together here at the Portland Police Bureau, have a good personal and professional relationship. We will coordinate all leads. When one of our team members gets relevant information about any of the cases, she and I will share it with each other, then pass it along to the group. No holds barred. We need to keep everyone in the loop 24/7. If you get something urgent, don't let it sit around until our next meeting."

Everyone headed off to their assignments when the meeting broke up, while Perez and Jansen stayed behind.

"Perez, you up for a walk?" Jansen asked. "I know this sweet little coffee shop about a half mile from here. We can take a streetcar if that's too much for you."

Perez gave Jansen a playful shoulder punch. "Better yet, let's go to Maya's Taqueria for Mexican and a cerveza."

"Now you're talking, " said Jansen. "By the way, Briggs filled me in on the Miller's party, the rare birds, and his videotape. He figured out that Colin Byrne is your other informant."

Perez nodded. "Jim's a superstar. Between Colin and Jim, our case is solid. We've got guys in Brazil and other locations working with federal officials to identify members of the bird poaching network. We're planning to arrest C-14 founders Jed and Lexi Miller. Once all the evidence and players are locked in, we'll execute a warrant."

"How long?" Jansen asked.

"You know how the Bureau works. Whatever we do involves a shitload of bureaucracy. That's why *Bureau* is our middle name."

Jansen chuckled.

"Weeks rather than days," said Perez.

At Maya's, they ordered street tacos and beer. "Here's to our new team," said Perez. "Let's enjoy some beers today. Then, tomorrow, we can begin kicking ass," said Jansen, her glass raised.

"Could Ginny Stanfield have killed her husband to prevent him from stopping the sale that would have set up the family for life?" Jansen asked.

"We picked up Mrs. Stanfield five or six days ago. You say the coroner figures he's been dead for about a week. The timeline fits."

"Meg McQuillan is also an obvious suspect," said Jansen. "She says she encouraged Stanfield to return the books. She also gave us a note from her dad, Bruce McQuillan, saying she would be getting another $900,000 on top of the $100,000 she found in his safe deposit."

"What was the source of the extra money?" Perez asked.

"The final sale of *The Birds of America* is a guess. We know McQuillan's Books was in financial trouble and that Meg gave up her dream job at the Portland

Central Library to help save the store. Maybe her dad promised her money from the sale. It's speculation, but I know it all ties together."

"Why don't I question Ginny Stanfield," said Perez. "I'll confront her with the affair and push on the money issue. After getting a court order to look at Stanfield's bank accounts, we found numerous small deposits—amounts in line with a slightly bigger-than-average paycheck. However, none of them hit the federal limit. As you know, the Bank Secrecy Act, updated in the Patriot Act in 2002, requires banks and credit unions to report consumer deposits of $10,000 or more.

"That fits with what Stanfield told Meg McQuillan," said Jansen.

"Jansen, it's been a slice of heaven visiting with you," Perez joked. "I'm going to a girlfriend's dinner party tonight. After that, I need to get home and clean up.

"Go," said Jansen. "I'll pay."

"Hoping you would offer to cover the bill," said Perez, smiling.

"Don't think I haven't noticed how often you get called away at the end of a meal, leaving me to pay," said Jansen.

Perez raised her eyebrows and smiled. "See you, Jansen."

CHAPTER 23

Jansen

1

Jansen finished her beer, paid the bill, and walked across the street to the streetcar stop. She caught the B Line, rode three stops, exited, and walked two blocks to her townhouse.

"What's happening?" Briggs asked when she walked into the kitchen.

"Just had a beer with Betty Perez. Talked about the new task force we established and how you're doing on the poaching case."

He looked at her, waiting for his grade.

"You get all A's," she said.

"What did you expect?"

Over dinner, Jansen filled Briggs in on the joint task force, her conversation with Perez, and her suspicions about Mrs. Stanfield and Meg McQuillan as murder suspects. "It hurts to see the pain in Larson's eyes when he considers the possibility. If I were Larson, I'd grab Meg and run off with her—take her to Sweden."

Briggs said he couldn't believe Meg was a suspect. "After what he went through with Helen and the potential loss of Meg, I wouldn't blame him for taking off," said Briggs. "Where does Dan McQuillan fit in this picture?"

"He appears to be a bystander. He was apparently on good terms with Bruce, assisted his brother with suicide, and was injured like the rest of us in the memorial shooting. According to Bruce's will, Dan is half-owner of McQuillan's Books, a nearly bankrupt company. What's there to gain? Why do you ask?"

"The other day, when Jed was briefing me on the details of the C-14 party ritual, he got a call from Lexi. I was standing close enough to hear her voice over the phone. He asked why she was meeting Dan at Andy's. I couldn't hear her answer. But her voice was loud, agitated. I've seen it first-hand. When Lexi gets annoyed, even at the smallest things, her voice jumps ten decibels."

"Are you sure you heard Jed say Dan?"

"I think so."

"Are you or aren't you sure?" said Jansen, like she was interviewing a suspect rather than talking to her husband. She scowled at him.

"Yes. I heard the name Dan."

Jansen closed her eyes, quiet for a minute, then opened them.

"Damn," she said. "I've now have third suspect in Stanfield's murder and an accomplice in the theft."

"Kim, I don't see Meg as a killer. She returned to the store to help her dad save the business. She had no guarantees of gaining anything. And everything to lose. As far as we know, she knew nothing about the money until after her dad died and she found the cash and note in the safe deposit box. As for Mrs. Stanfield, no doubt she was hurt and humiliated over the affair, but would she kill the father of their daughter? And, as you've said, their marriage was over when Meg got involved with him. Dan's my candidate for the killer of the day."

"You may be right."

Briggs offered, "Lexi is another likely killer. She is a trophy hunter who goes after rhinos and elephants."

"Now you're complicating my life," said Jansen.

"Here's another glass of wine. Drink it and relax. I guess you're rubbing off on me, Jansen," said Briggs. "I'm thinking like a detective."

"Better together," she said, fist-bumping him.

"Dinner's ready," he said.

They sat quietly, eating slowly, savoring the meal.

"Perfection, as usual," said Jansen. "You should change careers and become a chef."

"Cooking for you is chef enough, but thanks for the compliment."

2

The following day, Jansen arrived early at the police bureau and found Mark Larson at his desk.

"Chief, you want a cup of coffee?"

"What gives, Jansen? You're being too nice this morning—that's not you."

"Come on, Mark. I'm a pussycat, except when I'm not."

"Which is most of the time."

"Can't argue with that," she said, punching him lightly. "First, I wanted to tell you I'm crossing Meg off my suspect list."

Jansen explained her reasoning and the conversation she had with Briggs. She summarized her thoughts about Dan and how they could tie each case to him. Her briefing included a role for Lexi Miller in the theft and murder. Larson agreed they were making a solid case for a criminal conspiracy. Jansen agreed and outlined a likely crime scenario involving Dan McQuillan.

"Dan came on the scene long after the theft and disappearance of *The Birds of America*, but he had taken over store finances, filling in for his brother. Bruce could have made a deal to act as a go-between for Stanfield, the seller, and our unknown buyer. Once Bruce died, Dan could have taken over to complete the deal. According to Colin Byrne, Lexi desperately wanted a copy of the Audubon bird drawings. We know that Jed Miller bid $11 million to buy one at auction."

"And Dan could have known that and realized he could squeeze the Millers for more money," Larson added. "The warning to 'give me the damn bird book' could have come from Lexi."

"While Dan was trying to get more money—presumably for himself and Meg—he encountered Marc Stanfield, who wanted to call off the deal and give the books back," said Jansen.

"Were the four Audubon books in the safe?" asked Larson. "Did Dan lock up Stanfield and take the books? "

"It all fits," said Jansen. "But Brigg's account of hearing the name Dan mentioned in a phone call he overheard won't even get us close to locking down Dan McQuillan as the perpetrator."

"Let's not get crossways with Perez and her team," Larson said. "When we get something solid on the involvement of Dan and Lexi, give her a heads up."

"Will do. I'll brief the team."

3

Jansen called Detectives Munson, Berenson, and Millbrook into the incident room, filled them in on Perez's plans to interview Ginny Stanfield, their new suspect, and laid out Dan McQuillan's possible connection to the cases. "We think they all connect. Munson, we need you to call Andy at Andy's Firing Pen to verify if there was a meeting between Lexi and Dan." Munson nodded. "Will do, after breakfast. I've got this fat toasted coconut scone I picked up from Ovation this morning that's screaming Eat Me!"

Munson and Jansen had been at odds since Jansen had been promoted to detective. Although Jansen was a junior-grade detective, she was a hard charger. Munson was lazy, in Larson's judgment.

"I wouldn't dare get between you and your scone," said Jansen. "But could you eat and work?"

"Wouldn't be polite, would it?" said Munson, raising her eyebrows and smiling.

"Berenson, anything from Bill Bowman, director of the rare book room at the Central Library?"

"I put in a call to him. Left a message on his voicemail."

"Thanks," said Jansen. "Please call him back and tell him we need to check his logs for visits by Lexi Miller, Dan McQuillan, or Meg McQuillan. Focus on anyone who gave the reason for the visit as seeing *The Birds of America*.

"One more thing, guys. Report back whatever you find or don't find ASAP." They all nodded, including Munson.

CHAPTER 24

Meg

1

How could things get worse Meg wondered. Her dad was dead. Her uncle had shown up only a few weeks before, assisted dad with his suicide without telling her, then inherited half the bookstore. Mark said he loved her, but no doubt was having second thoughts. How could he marry a suspect in his murder case? Her dad's will had promised her $900,000. The Lottery? She knew it couldn't be legal.

Meg's chest tightened as she looked around her dad's apartment above the bookstore. She felt her life shrinking, marriage and a new life outside the bookstore slipping away. An unseen weight was crushing her like a car at a junkyard. She plopped down on Bruce's bed, which Dan mercifully had made with clean sheets. The blanket was tight, and the corners neatly tucked, like you would expect from an ex-soldier like Dan.

Bruce's apartment was as cluttered as the store downstairs, overflowing with books. Why didn't he grab a book as needed rather than bring them upstairs and throw them down wherever he found a spot? He had turned into a packrat. Then there was a shelf behind his pillow, with books neatly lined up. Meg fiddled with her ponytail, then moved her hand to the bandage on her cheek. The eye was itching like an infected mosquito bite. She wanted to rip off the tape and dig her nails into the offending spot. Instead, she moved her hand away, pressed on the tape to make sure it stuck, and looked closer at her dad's book choices.

All were first editions, a gamut of fiction and non-fiction. Atwood. LaMott. King. Child. Strayed. Proulx. Lahiri. Stroud. And a rare title she knew about from the 1920s but had never seen: *One of Ours* by Willa Cather. There were at least 50 titles on two shelves, all in perfect condition. A few were extremely rare.

Although Meg considered the possibility her dad was involved in *The Birds of America* theft and sale, she wanted to think the best of him. So she pushed her doubts aside as she continued to scan the bookshelf. The private collection in his bedroom, besides the rare books they had elsewhere in McQuillan's, would have a total value of $200,000, she estimated. Still, a long way from the $900,000 dad said promise. She must have missed something.

Meg pulled Annie Proulx's *Shipping News*, her dad's favorite of all time, from the shelf and read a few pages. She was pushing the book back in the tightly-packed row of books when she saw a black leather-bound journal tucked behind. She reached in and pulled it out. There was no name on the cover. She opened it and saw her dad's handwriting, *The Personal Journal of Bruce James McQuillan.*

Her dad's handwriting was neat, the letters small and precise. He'd perfected his cursive penmanship as a boy in Scotland—no doubt the result of nuns looking over his shoulder, making corrections or rapping him on the knuckles with a ruler for every mistake. He practiced all his life, often sending handwritten notes and letters to friends. Finally, about three-fourths of the way through the journal pages, Meg came to the last page containing notes. All alone on a page, the final words were a plea: "Please don't judge me harshly or hate me. I did what I did for your future. You deserve everything good you get. I will always love you—in my heart and in your dreams."

Meg burst into tears. "I could never hate you," she said, looking at the end page. "You will always be my hero." After she was cried out, she started reading the last chapter, twenty detailed pages before the ending inscription.

The final pages of the journal were a litany of regrets. "I should have closed the store after your mom died, sold the inventory, and invested the money. Instead, I selfishly hung on. I wasn't ready for retirement and was afraid that I would have no place to go and nothing to do. I felt I had no choice."

The following passages described how Bruce McQuillan met Marc Stanfield when he visited the library's rare book room and discussed the preservation and sale of rare books. Bruce showed off McQuillan's small treasure trove of prize books to Stanfield. Weeks later, kicked out of his house and lonely, Stanfield asked Bruce to have a beer with him. He admitted that books and alcohol were his only company. Next, Stanfield began pouring out his family and money problems, talking to Bruce like the good father Stanfield claimed he never had. Finally, over several months and lots of beer, Stanfield revealed his plan to rescue himself and his family from impending financial ruin. Bruce, facing his own financial doomsday, jumped at it.

Stanfield had paid a janitor to move the four-volume set of *The Birds of America* to the library's trash pickup area late one night, where they transferred them to Stanfield's car. Stanfield took them to McQuillan's and he and Bruce agreed to hide them in the basement safe.

Realizing that he could drop dead of a heart attack at any moment, Bruce gave Stanfield the combination. They agreed they would wait at least six months or more until the cops, unable to solve the case, would move on. They also agreed that Stanfield, who quickly became the chief suspect, should disappear. Even if the police couldn't arrest him, the library board could fire him and make him fall guy for the library's loss. On the day of his disciplinary hearing, Stanfield disappeared with Bruce's help. Bruce used his contacts to get Stanfield a forged driver's license, rent a small room, and have enough money to get started until he could find a job.

Bruce also wrote that Stanfield gave him the name of a potential buyer and Bruce followed up. The buyer provided a 20 percent down payment on the $2 million asking price and agreed to wait the six months until the seller was ready to complete the deal. "I kept $100,000 and gave Marc the other half," Bruce wrote.

In the next to last paragraph before signing off, Bruce wrote, "Uncle Dan has agreed to work with the buyer and Stanfield to complete the deal. He knows all the details and has access to the safe." The journal did not reveal the name of the buyer.

2

Meg lay down on the bed and pulled the pillow over her face. The smell of her dad's Old Spice aftershave, which she loved, permeated. If her eye injury and affair with Stanfield hadn't finished a future with Larson, her dad's involvement in the theft would.

She knew she had to face up to the reality of losing everything. She was also damn mad at Uncle Dan. She pulled out her phone, called him, and got voicemail. "Call me immediately," Meg demanded, cold as ice. Her next call was to Mark.

Larson picked up the call on the first ring. "Sweetheart, how are you?"

"Never more miserable," she answered. "My life is over."

"What's the matter?"

"I just discovered that Dad kept a journal. He admits to conspiring with Marc Stanfield to steal and sell *The Birds of America*. He also said he asked Dan to take over the final negotiations. So that's how I was going to get $900,000. Can you imagine me benefitting from books stolen from a public library—a place I love and a job I treasured?"

"I know you would never steal from a library," he said. "Stay where you are. I'll be right over. But whatever you do, don't call Dan or alert him. Your life could be in danger."

"What are you talking about?" she said.

"Dan is about to get a big payday and go on his way—away from the bookstore. Like you suggested, he never gave a rip about working there. He just came home for Bruce's death, no doubt, and to see what he could squeeze out in an inheritance."

"I just called Dan and left him a voice mail. I demanded he call me ASAP. I didn't say why."

"Listen to me, Meg. Get the gun under the counter and keep the door locked."

"Let me look for the gun before you hang up." She found the gun under the cash register where they always kept it.

"Mark, I have the gun. I'm alone, and Uncle Dan could come back any moment. Hurry."

"Stand near the store entrance but keep the gun hidden. I'll be there in five minutes."

CHAPTER 25

Jansen

1

"Jansen, this is Munson. Andy gave me some interesting news. He said Dan and Lexi were at the Firing Pen two days ago, shooting up a storm with high-powered rifles. They both appeared angry, alternately firing at targets like they were trying to impress each other. After about 30 minutes, they packed up their rifles and stood face-to-face, inches apart. They were talking intensely. Andy said the sound from other shooters drowned out the conversation. When they left, they politely thanked him, said they would return soon. Then they walked out to their cars in the parking lot."

"Did they drive off together?" Jansen asked.

"No. Andy said they moved their cars side-by-side and opened their trunks. Dan removed a large package, about three feet by four feet, and put it into Lexi's SUV. Then they both drove off. But there's more, which may be a break in our cases. Andy said Dan McQuillan is a legendary ex-Army sniper with over 50 kills. The gun he used at the range was the same one he carried in the war. Dan's commanding officer felt Dan deserved it like a trophy you could put on the mantle."

"Hardly something you could brag about," Jansen said.

"Andy also said Lexi regularly fires the .600 Nitro ammo found at the memorial shooting. The day of the memorial Lexi was not at the range."

"Munson, I underestimated your investigative abilities," said Jansen. "You get all A's today."

"Thanks, Teach!" Munson said sarcastically.

125

2

Just as Jansen hung up, Larson stood at the side of her desk. "Let's go. Meg just called, and I think she's in danger. I'll explain on the road."

Jansen jumped up and followed Larson to his car. He threw the lights and siren on top and raced out of the police bureau parking lot.

"Tell me what's happening, Mark."

"Meg called and said she found her father's journal detailing how he and Marc Stanfield conspired to steal the Audubon books. There's also evidence Dan McQuillan is involved and may have taken over the sale of the books. Evidently, the money Meg was expecting would come from the sale. Meg wants no part of it and left a voicemail for Dan to call her. She didn't tell him why she was calling but said it was urgent. Her life may be in danger if he suspects she's on to him."

"Munson called me and said Lexi Miller and Dan McQuillan were at Andy's Firing Pen a couple days ago," said Jansen. "They appeared locked in a battle over who was the deadliest shot, each with a high-powered rifle. Lexi was using an elephant gun and Dan a sniper rifle, according to Andy. Afterward, they went to the parking lot where Dan transferred a large object to Lexi's car. I think it was one of the Audubon books."

3

When Jansen and Larson pulled up to McQuillan's Books, they were barely out of the car when Meg ran outside, crying, spinning, and waving a gun. Larson and Jansen froze.

"Meg, it's okay," said Larson. "Please set the gun down. Someone will get hurt."

"Everyone I know is getting hurt," Meg cried. "Maybe I should hurt myself."

"Meg," said Jansen, "You need a hug, not a gun." Jansen walked over, pulled the gun from her trembling hand, and hugged her.

"Jump in here, Larson." Jansen moved back and let Larson talk Meg down and comfort her. "I know it's a shock," he said. "You've been through a lot these past few days. You'll be okay. I'll help you through it." When she stopped crying, The bandage on Meg's injured eye was soaked with tears.

"Dan was just here," said Meg. "He came out of nowhere. He must have been in the office working. I told him I knew what he was doing and that he needed to stop. I waved the journal, then threw it on Dad's bed. Despite what the journal said, Dan claimed he didn't know what I was talking about. He suggested Dad's mind was playing tricks on him."

"Leave it to us," said Jansen. "First, let's have a look at the journal."

The three of them walked up to Bruce McQuillan's apartment above the store.

"It's gone," said Meg. "Dan must have taken it."

"Is he still in the store?"

"He said he had errands to run and would be back in a couple of hours, then could talk about Dad, the journal, and the store's future. So he left, and I came downstairs to meet you."

"Did you point the gun at him?" Larson asked.

"Yes. I aimed it at him and told him to come clean, or I would shoot. He said it wasn't loaded."

"He's right," said Jansen. "I checked it out the last time I was here. Bruce apparently didn't want to kill anyone, just scare them."

"How did Dan know it wasn't loaded?" Larson asked.

"He must have seen it behind the counter," said Meg. "Dad said Dan was a sharpshooter in the Army. He knows everything about guns."

"She's right," said Jansen. "Anyone familiar with firearms will check first to see if it's loaded. It's Gun Safety 101."

"We'll find him," said Larson. "Meanwhile, I'll get a uniformed officer to keep an eye out for Dan here. Will you be okay until the officer arrives?"

"I'll be fine. If Dan returns before I hear from you, I'll text you a thumbs-up.

"I'll see you later, Meg," said Larson. "Don't worry so much. Things will be okay. I promise." He kissed her and then left with Jansen.

"Could he have used the gun, loaded or not, to force Marc Stanfield into the safe?" Jansen asked.

"It's possible," said Larson. "He could have purchased ammo or pretended it was loaded. An experienced military shooter, like Dan, could have been very convincing for someone like Stanfield, a librarian who probably had no experience with firearms."

"None of it matters now without the journal," said Jansen. "We've got to get it before Dan destroys it."

CHAPTER 26

Dan

1

"Lexi, this is Dan. Urgent that you call me regarding the remaining bird books."

Dan purposely left the message vague, attempting to keep his voice neutral. He was not a panicker. Instead, he relied on his training as a sniper to deal with stress: relax, slow his breathing and heart rate, and focus on the target. Once he collected his payout, Meg could keep the decrepit, failing bookstore. He would, of course, deposit the money Bruce promised Meg. But she wouldn't get half of the book sale proceeds. She would get a fourth. What she didn't know wouldn't hurt her. He could escape to some remote destination with a enough cash to live the high life until he died.

On the coffee table in front of him was one of books of Audubon's paintings he would soon deliver to Lexi. He opened it, felt the rich texture of the paper, and studied the images. The images were dazzling. Although he had no emotional connection with the books or any interest in owning them, he was impressed that he was looking at work created 200 years earlier. He knew Lexi would protect them with her life. That fact alone relieved any guilt he might have had about their being stolen property.

He closed the book, returned it to the protective covering Stanfield had provided, and picked up Bruce's journal. If he hadn't snatched it from Meg, he would already be on the run, under arrest—and penniless. His first instinct was the tear out and burn the pages confirming his involvement in the conspiracy. But, instead, he would keep the journal. Then, after he was out of the country, safely ensconced with ready access to a few million dollars, he would mail it to

Meg. She had a right to her father's words and the truth about his life and final days.

Dan tucked the journal into his travel bag, prepared to leave on a moment's notice. While he looked over the bag's contents to ensure it held his travel essentials, including his passport, bank book, and cash, a call lit up his phone. He didn't recognize the number. Was it Lexi on a burner phone or a spam call? He couldn't take a chance of missing Lexi's call.

"Dan McQuillan," he said.

"Dan, this is Detective Kim Jansen, Meg's friend."

"How can I help you, Detective?" His voice had turned from welcoming to ice cold when he realized who was calling.

"We were just with Meg. She said you were here a couple of hours ago and took her father's journal, which puts you in the middle of *The Birds of America* theft. So, we'd like you to come in and talk to us."

"Detective Jansen, I would love to spend the afternoon drinking coffee with you and catching up. Unfortunately, I have a busy day. I know nothing about a journal. I'm not sure you can trust Meg's memory. She's been under a lot of stress. Maybe she's imagining it, hoping to learn more about her Dad's decision to die and his thoughts about her future." While trying to decide what to say next, his phone vibrated.

"Got a call coming in," he said. "Let's talk later. Bye. " He recognized the incoming call as spam. The timing was perfect. He didn't want appear to just hang up on Jansen, reinforcing her suspicions, but needed to talk to Lexi. She picked up after a half dozen rings.

"Sorry, Dan, I was in my studio," she said. "What's going on?"

"Lexi, my brother kept a diary in which he outlined his deal with Marc Stanfield. He finished writing it just before he died and said I would be completing the deal. My niece Meg found it and called me. I was already in the store in the office working on the financials. I walked up to my brother's apartment and talked to her. I tried to assure her everything was legitimate and that the books we were selling were not those stolen from the library. But, unfortunately, she's not buying it."

"You need to get that journal or we're all screwed," said Lexi.

"Relax, I got it. When Meg went to the bathroom, I grabbed the journal and left. You're not mentioned anywhere. Without the journal, there's only hearsay. We're in the clear."

"What's the next move?" she asked. "I can't lose the books."

"You won't. I'll load the remaining three into the car in about two minutes and drive to your place. But before I deliver them, I need to verify payment has been wired."

"I just completed the transfer, minus the $200,000 down payment. You should find a deposit of $3.8 million."

"Hold on while I check," he said. Dan walked to his laptop, logged into his account, and confirmed the deposit. He logged off, picked up his phone, and said, "In 15 minutes, I'll be on my way to your place with the books. This will be a quick exchange."

2

Dan loaded the last three volumes of *The Birds of America* for delivery to Lexi, then returned to his apartment to get his travel case and documents. He looked around. Good riddance to this one-bedroom shithole. His life had been filled with dirty hotels and dreary apartments as he traveled worldwide on the cheap. This was probably the worst, in the rainy Pacific Northwest, one flight above a garbage-filled street lined with tents occupied by some of Portland's 4,000 homeless. Keeping his costs to a minimum had allowed him more travel. Walking through the detritus was a small price to pay for freedom. Thankfully, he would be leaving it behind for the beauty and warmth of someplace tropical. He'd fly to Australia, then go from there, the perfect launching pad for adventures in the South Pacific, Indonesia, and more.

He put the bag over his shoulder, walked to the front door, and opened it.

"Hello, Uncle Dan. Going someplace?"

Pointed at his belly was his brother's 18-shot American Ruger.

What was she thinking, coming at him twice with the same unloaded gun? He should have taken it with him after she aimed it at him two hours earlier. With a sweep of his hand, he snatched the gun and pulled her inside.

"Are you crazy? A loaded gun kills."

"Yes, the gun is loaded, and killing you and your buyer is what I had in mind. I know you killed Marc so you could get your grimy hands on the Audubon books. You'd undoubtedly take the money and run, leaving me high and dry."

"You've got it all wrong. I didn't kill anyone." Dan figured he could convince her that Lexi was the culprit if need be.

"When Bruce told me Stanfield was planning to return the books, I got the combination, opened the safe, and moved them here for safekeeping. I never saw Marc or talked to him. I've never met him. I followed your Dad's wishes to see the sale through at all costs. But not at the cost of murder."

"I don't believe you. A few hours ago, you said you knew nothing about a deal. Now, you've changed your story."

"Okay, I lied. I wanted to keep you out of this mess."

"Either way, they should go back to the library where they belong," said Meg, crossing her arms defiantly. "All you care about is the money," she said, pouting.

"Right or wrong—and I can't say I am comfortable with people stealing from the public library—Bruce made a deal with the devil. The devil was Marc Stanfield, desperate for money for his wife and daughter and a new life for himself. Stanfield pitched the idea to your Dad to hold on to the books for six months until the brouhaha settled down about the theft and that insurance paid off the library. Bruce said Stanfield had a buyer in mind when he came up with the plan."

"Who's the buyer?"

"Doesn't matter, does it? I am about to deliver the last three of the four books. The money has been deposited into my account. In a few days, you'll get what your Dad promised."

"I don't want dirty money."

"When the money appears in your account, and you realize you can escape from that mess once proudly known as McQuillan's Books, you won't care if the money is covered with shit. You'll take it and run. Think about it. You can go anywhere, do anything. Go back to the library and get the job you always wanted, unconcerned about money for everyday expenses."

"I want to meet the buyer, or I'm calling Mark Larson and Kim Jansen, revealing the entire scheme. You'll never make it out of town."

Dan's body sagged. He knew Meg wasn't going to let up. He'd have to involve Lexi.

"I give up," said Dan. "You win. Let's go meet the buyer. As far as I know, the buyer had nothing to do with Stanfield's death. Just remember, your father was a good man who had a last wish—for you to have a way to escape the crumbling bookstore that's gobbled up three generations of McQuillans. Yes, it provided a living for the early generations. Now it's a living, dark thing. You need to escape before it kills you." Meg was silent.

"Let's meet the buyer and put your fears to rest." Dan led her to the car and headed off to the Miller Estate.

CHAPTER 27

Larson

Mark Larson called Meg and got her voicemail. A perky voice said she would call back 'before the sun sets.' Cute, Larson thought. Where was she?

Jansen walked into his office.

"We've got a team call set up in fifteen minutes, at 10 a.m. Betty will share the results of her interview with Ginny Stanfield and what they've found in the Stanfield bank accounts. We'll give her what we've got and create a joint response plan. We both think we can make arrests before the end of the day and close one or two of our cases."

"Great," said Larson, who had been looking out the window when she walked in. He stayed that way while she talked.

"What's going on?" Jansen asked. "You look like you've checked out. I thought you'd be happy to see this mess wrapping up."

"I'm worried about Meg, especially with Dan McQuillan in the wind."

"Meg is resourceful. She'll be careful and let us know if she's in danger. Remember, she said she would text you if she encounters Dan."

"Excuse me, Boss," said Detective Millbrook, "Bill Bowman confirmed that a Lexicon Ann Miller visited the library 17 times over six months. Each time she viewed *The Birds of America*. Her profession is listed as *artist* on the visitor record. Her reason for visiting was to study Audubon's painting style."

"Great work, Millbrook," said Larson.

"We now have links between Stanfield and Lexi Miller," said Jansen. "We know Jed Miller tried and failed to buy a copy of *The Birds of America* at an auction. And we have confirmation she and Dan McQuillan know each other. In addition, Lexi owns high-powered rifles and is an expert shot. Combine that with what Meg said was in her dad's journal, and I see a case building for theft and murder."

"We have a lot of smoke and mirrors," said Larson, who swung his chair around and faced Jansen and Millbrook, who was standing in the doorway of Larson's office. "Where's Bruce McQuillan's journal? Where's Dan? What is his role in the debacle? Where are the bird books? And where the hell is Meg?"

"We need to get to the conference room for the call," said Jansen. "Perez might have some answers."

With the team gathered and the call connected, Perez reported on her interview with Ginny Stanfield.

"After we told Mrs. Stanfield we had seen her bank records, she admitted her husband had been sending her money each month to keep her and her daughter afloat," said Perez. "She frequently took trips to visit him in Eastern Oregon, where he was hiding. Her husband pleaded for forgiveness and admitted his affair with Meg McQuillan, which she said she knew about. And, get this, Stanfield confessed to what he called a 'brief fling' with Lexi Miller. Mrs. Stanfield believes Lexi used those occasions to plant the idea for *The Birds of America* theft."

"I also have something for you," said Jansen. "Meg McQuillan found her father's journal which details the theft conspiracy. According to the journal, Stanfield and McQuillan became drinking buddies, commiserating over financial problems. Eventually, they came up with the idea to steal the bird paintings. It also mentions that Dan McQuillan recently learned about the deal and agreed to his brother Bruce's dying request to complete the sale."

"That's dynamite," said Perez. "The journal is golden. So, you've got it, right?"

"There's the rub. Meg called us about the journal, upset that her Uncle Dan had been lying to her. She's sure he killed Stanfield to prevent him from returning the books to the library. Before we got to the store, Dan appeared and she confronted him. He denied everything. When she went to the bathroom, Dan apparently snatched the journal and took off."

"Looks to me like Lexi Miller is the buyer, and Dan McQuillan is the seller," Detective Munson said. "If we want to find Dan, Lexi, and the books, we go to the Miller house. I'll bet we'll find them there."

"Where's Meg?" Perez said.

"She isn't answering her phone," said Larson. "I've called three times and no pickup. That's not like her."

"I think it's time to move on the Millers," said Perez. We've got them on our poaching case. Their contacts in South America have been arrested and are talking. I agree with Detective Munson that the Miller Estate is ground zero."

"I agree," said Larson.

"Perez, hold a minute," said Jansen. "Jim is supposed to be there this afternoon tending to the birds in their aviary. I can track his phone." Jansen logged into PupFinder, a canine tracking website, and found him right where she expected.

"I checked, and he is at the house. In case you all don't know him, he's six-foot-six with a shock of red hair and a red beard. So, when we get there, and you see this big guy who looks like a Viking, he's my husband, not a suspect."

"Let's get our SWAT commanders in touch to organize a raid," Perez suggested.

"Good idea," said Larson. "Will these hotshots be able to work together?"

"As I understand it," said Perez, "your SWAT leader Bull Harrison, and ours, Amy Clark, are ex-military and they've worked successfully on other cases."

"How long until launch?" asked Larson.

"Best case, 90 minutes," Perez said.

"Great," said Larson. "We'll alert our guys and tell him to move their asses."

"Remember, Jim Briggs is on site," said Jansen. "Meg McQuillan may also be there. If you haven't met Meg, she's a five-foot-seven brunette with a ponytail. She looks like she's about to go camping. Long-sleeve flannel shirts are her trademark. Lexi Miller is a fiery redhead with creamy white skin. There shouldn't be an I.D. problem."

CHAPTER 28

Meg

1

Lexi heard the buzz from the security gate and walked over to a touch screen to see who was there. She recognized Dan McQuillan, but not the woman passenger. "Who's in the car with you, and why is she here?" she texted Dan.

"My niece, Meg. She insisted I bring her to meet with you or she would call the police. She wants to return the books to the library. I'm certain we can talk her out of it and complete our agreement." He didn't mention that Meg was Stanfield's ex-lover and Portland Police Bureau Chief Detective Mark Larson's fiancée. A moment later, the gate opened and Dan drove to the front door.

Dan knocked and waited for Lexi to open the door. Instead, an electronic latch retracted, and the front door swung open enough for them to enter. A woman's voice over a speaker instructed them to walk to the hallway's end and enter the first door on the right.

Meg was in awe of the Miller home's splendor, size, and massive amounts of Italian marble. An array of speakers filled the house with the sweet sound of birds singing. She felt like she was walking through a forest, with murals depicting vivid scenes from the Amazon.

When they arrived at Lexi Miller's art gallery, Meg was again stunned by the beauty, especially the wall art, a pantheon of beautiful birds.

"I understand you wanted to meet," said Lexi, who appeared from the back of the room, coming out from behind a curtain. It was as if the Wizard of Oz was revealing himself. But, instead, a stunning redhead stood a few feet from Meg. "You're the buyer?" asked Meg.

"That's me," said Lexi.

"Why do you want the Audubon books?"

"I'm an artist who intends to create the most beautiful bird book ever. I'll use Audubon's books as a guide to improve my paintings. Soon, the critics will hold up my work side-by-side and declare mine superior. Audubon's work will fade into history."

Unlikely, Meg thought. The woman is delusional.

"I don't care about your dream. You're a killer. You're going to jail. The books are going back to the library."

"I never said Lexi killed Marc Stanfield," said Dan. "I said I didn't do it. Your Dad may have done it, for all we know."

"Dad would never kill a person over a book sale, even at the risk of losing the store."

"Dan, tell her," Lexi said. "Tell her the truth—you killed Marc when he wanted to return the stolen books."

Meg turned and glared at Dan. "Is that true?"

Dan said nothing.

"You may not know that your uncle was an Army sniper, killing people from thousands of yards away. He's legendary for his 50 kills. They never knew what hit them. And Marc Stanfield didn't have a chance."

Dan took a deep breath. "The men and women I killed were enemy combatants. We killed them before they could kill us."

"You killed Marc?" Meg's eyes went wide, a grimace exposing clenched teeth. "I knew it." Dan glared at her.

"Are you sure you want the truth?"

"How much more could you hurt me? Just tell me the truth."

Should he tell her that her Dad's dying words were a confession that he had killed Stanfield, desperately trying to protect Meg's future? Bruce had given the Audubon Books to Dan for safekeeping after removing them from the safe.

No, Dan wouldn't soil Meg's memory of her Dad. Bruce had stayed in the trenches at the bookstore while Dan traveled the world. It was time for Dan to pay his debt to his big brother. He had to lie.

"I had no choice. I gave Stanfield several chances to change his mind. He wouldn't listen to reason. I intended to leave him there for an hour. When I returned to see if he had changed his mind, he was dead. He ran out of air before I could come back. It was an accident."

Meg turned to Lexi. "You and Dan are both going to jail for murder and conspiracy. I don't know what other charges they'll come up with, but you'll both be locked up forever."

"I don't think so," said Lexi, pulling a pistol from the pocket of her paint-covered apron.

"No!" Meg yelled, lunging for the pistol. For the next few seconds, she and Lexi wrestled for control. Meg tried to use both hands to twist the gun away. Lexi was shoving at Meg. When the gun went off, a scream filled the room. They looked over and saw Dan crumpling to the floor, holding his stomach.

"Damn you," said Dan. "Look what you've done." He could barely squeeze out the words. "Lexi, you've killed the deal, and probably me. So now, who's the fucking killer?"

"I'm sorry, Uncle Dan," Meg cried. "Forgive me." She looked at Lexi. "Do something. Call an ambulance. We have to save him."

Still holding the gun, Lexi said, "Dan, I paid you $4 million for *Birds of America*. I'll have a complete set between the books in your trunk and the volume I have. So, I got what I wanted, and you're getting the untimely death you deserve, you greedy bastard."

Meg got up and walked to Lexi. "He's dying. Get help."

"Get back, or you're going to get a bullet, too," Lexi said. Then, as Meg backed away, Jim Briggs came around the corner. Briggs looked at Dan on the floor, then Meg, whose face was a mask of fear, and the gun in Lexi's hand.

"Lexi, put that down," said Briggs. "You'll hurt someone else."

She laughed. "This was all supposed to be so simple: Stanfield steals the books, then I get the books six months later. I even slept with him to seal the deal. I'm the one who suggested he consider stealing them. He was such a sad sack. Bruce McQuillan offered the books to me for $2 million. Dan got greedy and squeezed Jed and me for twice that."

Waving the gun between Briggs and Meg, Lexi walked over to a large door, entered a combination in the electric lock, and pulled it open. Inside was the Miller's safe room. The room was filled with food, water, cots, lights, personal items, and medical supplies—enough for a month.

"Drag Dan in here," Lexi said, pointing her gun at Briggs.

"We need to get Dan to the hospital," said Briggs. "He needs emergency surgery."

"Not going to happen," said Lexi. "Move! Now."

Jim got under Dan's arms and dragged him into the safe room, his limp body leaving a trail of blood. Dan screamed with pain as Briggs moved him.

"Meg, you get in there, too."

"I'm not going," she said.

"The alternative is for me to shoot you and let Jim drag your bloody body inside, too," Lexi said.

"Do what she says, Meg," said Briggs. "She shoots elephants for a hobby."

When Meg was inside, Lexi leaned in and said, "Jim, I don't care what happens to Dan. He's a swindler and extortionist. But I don't want to hurt Meg. I suspect she didn't know about the extra extra money Dan squeezed out of us."

"He promised me $900,000," said Meg. "He acted as if that was fifty percent of the total coming from the sale."

"Dan is going to die if we don't get him to the hospital," Briggs repeated.

"Throw your cell phones out here, now," Lexi demanded. Briggs took his and Meg's and slid them on the floor out the door opening.

"Get Dan's," she said.

"It's in my pocket," Dan said, barely able to speak from the pain. "You've got to help me. I'm bleeding out."

"You're lower than a stray dog," said Lexi. "Jim can use his veterinary skills to patch you up. There are medical supplies in that brown bag in the corner." With that, she closed the door and hit the lock button, then picked up the phones, including Dan's, slick with blood.

"Let us out," came Meg's muffled cry, followed by pounding on the door.

2

As Meg continued to pound, Lexi thought she should take Meg hostage, insurance that she and Jed could escape. They would go to an oceanfront home they bought in the Philippines for $150,000. The house had been a distress sale by an American writer who had built the mansion as his retirement dream. After a cyclone killed members of the man's family and wrecked the house, he returned to the U.S. In less than a year, Lexi and Jed had resurrected it to its original glory, massive glass windows looking over a vast sea—a perfect place to perfect her painting technique. Once out of the reach of law enforcement, they could stay in touch with the Red Flock and meet them for annual birding trips.

But, if she left Meg behind and Dan died, Lexi could claim she knew nothing about the source of the books. There was no law against purchasing rare books. Of course, holding three people against their will and preventing a wounded man from getting emergency care might raise a few eyebrows. But she knew what she had to do.

Lexi dialed the unlock code and stood back as the door opened. Meg, who had been pushing against the door, flew out and landed face-first on the floor. Lexi closed the door and locked it, ignoring another plea from Briggs to get help for Dan.

"Get up, Meg, we're leaving. We need to go *now*."

"I've got to get out of here," Lexi said to her dog, Trudy, who was cowering in the corner from the gunshot and struggle. "It's okay, girl. I can't take you where we're going, but you'll be okay."

Lexi knew she had to leave and could never come back. She would never see Trudy again or her beautiful home. Undoubtedly, the police would soon find Briggs and issue a manhunt for her.

Lexi aimed her gun at Meg and said to follow her. When they got to Lexi's studio, she pulled out a roll of duct tape. "Put your hands out." Meg extended them in front of her and let Lexi bind them.

"It's too tight."

"Live with it," said Lexi. "Shut up and follow me. I'm leaving and you're going with me." Meg stopped as if she was going to resist. Lexi grabbed her roughly by the arm and dragged her along.

Meg stood in the driveway watching as Lexi put *The Birds of America* books into the back of her Range Rover. Next Lexi threw in a small suitcase, helped Meg into the back seat, and closed the door. Lexi returned to the house to get her elephant gun, two handguns, and ammo boxes. The rifle was the same weapon she had used to blow apart Bruce McQuillan's memorial urn. Finally, she pulled on her jacket and gloves. A storage shed near East Lake housed the snowmobile, ski clothes, and extra supplies for winter trips to the snowbound cabin that they would need.

Given the recent snowy weather—a 50-year record for Portland and the nearby Cascade Mountains—there would be plenty of snow. She would need the snowmobile to carry weapons and at least one Audubon book. She would store the others away in the climate-controlled shed.

Lexi knew time was running out. She looked at her home in all its splendor: the murals, art gallery, studio, aviary filled with rare birds, and so much more. Leaving her Tanager behind was a stab to the heart. So beautiful. The best birthday present ever.

Lexi was about to climb into the car when she remembered one more thing she needed: hers and Jed's 'celebration' costumes with bird masks and his BB gun. She found all three, ran back to the car, opened the trunk and placed them on top of her suitcase.

She was at the gate a moment later, hit her electronic opener and headed out. The trip to East Lake was two hours if the roads were open. As she waited for the gate to open, she texted Jed: "I'm heading to the cabin. Don't tell anyone where I am. I'll explain later. Come as soon as you can."

CHAPTER 29

Jansen

SWAT Commanders Bull Harrison, a Portland policeman, and Amy Clark, an FBI agent, pulled their teams together and alerted Jansen and Perez that the assembly point for the raid would be in Washington Park, near the Sacajawea statue. Thirty minutes later, SWAT and the task force members had assembled, ready for the raid.

Harrison and Clark stood on the grass next to the statue for the briefing. "Listen up, everyone," said Harrison. "We'll park near the Miller's front gate. Clark's team will have two men advance to the gate and breach it. Once the gate is open, we'll surround the house. FBI Agents and Portland detectives will provide backup. Once we make entry and secure the scene, task force members can enter. Uniformed officers and a fire paramedic unit will be standing by. There may be hostages, and one or more armed suspects, so stay alert."

"One of our suspects," said Jansen, "is Lexi Miller. She's a redhead with light skin. She also is a champion pistol shooter and big game hunter. She owns and shoots big guns with powerful ammo."

"Finally," Perez added. "Detective Jansen's husband, Jim Briggs, is undercover, working as a veterinarian for our suspects. Det. Jansen has pinpointed his location in the house through a GPS device Briggs carries on his keychain. You can't miss him. He's six-feet-six with red hair and a red beard. Dresses like a surfer with Hawaiian shirts, shorts, and sandals. He's one of the ours. Questions?" No one responded.

"Everyone ready?" Clark asked. When she confirmed nods from every team member, she said, "Let's move. And one more thing, this park is full of hikers, joggers, and tourists visiting the rose gardens and the Holocaust memorial. Proceed with caution."

Moving in tight formation, vehicles just a few feet apart, SWAT was at the front gate of the Miller estate in less than five minutes. A minute later, SWAT had opened the gate and surrounded the house, entering from the front and back.

The rear-entry team found itself in the aviary. The heat and humidity were what you'd expect in a South American forest, but not the West Hills of Portland in winter. The cacophony of bird sounds drowned out their footsteps. They tried to ignore the flapping wings and stay focused on the entry door to the main house ahead.

The front entry team moved down the long entry hallway, then into the gallery of bird paintings. Finally, when both teams had finished sweeping the massive home, Clark and Harrison each signaled all clear.

Moments later, Jansen and Perez were in the residence, moving toward the location of Briggs' GPS signal. They stopped in front of a large door.

"He's in here," said Jansen. "Jim, can you hear me?"

"I hear you," a faint male voice answered.

"Harrison, can you breach this door?"

He looked at it. "It's hardened steel," he said, tapping the butt of his AR-15 on the door. "My guess is that this is a safe room." He pointed to a keypad to the right of the door. "Short of blowing off the hinges and injuring the occupants, we would need to cut it open with a torch. That could take hours. Getting the entry code would be safer and faster."

Mark Larson took control. "Jed Miller is a heart surgeon at OHSU Hospital. We checked earlier today and learned he was scheduled to perform a triple bypass. My guess is there is a procedure to interrupt him in an emergency. This is one of those times. Lt. Harrison, please take care of it. You know those guys and can light a fire under them. Don't tell them too much. Say we have a repairman who accidentally locked himself in the safe room at the Miller residence and we need to get him out ASAP."

Thirty minutes later, the code was transmitted to Harrison, who used it to open the door. He stood back as Jansen and Larson rushed in.

"We need an ambulance," said Briggs, pointing to a blood-soaked bandage covering Dan McQuillan's stomach. "I found some painkillers in the stash of medical supplies. But, with his gut shot, it's not nearly enough."

"Where's Meg?" Larson asked.

"Lexi put her in here, then let her out. Lexi must have her."

"There's an ambulance crew coming down the hallway," said Jansen.

"Over here," Perez yelled. The paramedics and an emergency physician entered the room. "Beverly Brockton is one of the trauma chiefs at OHSU. She'll take over. A chopper is nearby to take him to the medical center."

Brockton and Briggs spoke briefly about what he'd done to stabilize Dan. At the same time, paramedics rolled Dan onto a stretcher, lifted it to waist height, and moved it out the door.

"What happened?" Jansen asked Briggs.

"I was in the aviary caring for the birds when I heard a loud noise coming from Lexi's studio. I ran over there, found Dan on the floor and Meg yelling at Lexi. She said Dan admitted killing Marc Stanfield, locking him in the safe to prevent him from returning *The Birds of America* to the library. I thought Meg might have shot Dan. But Lexi was holding the gun, while Meg demanded Lexi turn herself in and give the books back."

Briggs filled in Jansen on the rest of the exchange between Lexi, Dan, and Meg. Lexi admitted firing the shot at the memorial. She was upset that Dan had doubled the price Bruce and Lexi had agreed on. Since he was locked in the saferoom, he had no idea where Lexi took Meg.

Jansen turned to Perez. "We're close, but still need more evidence to lock down our cases," she said. "We need Lexi."

"We called the hospital and learned that Jed Miller finished surgery a half hour ago and was not in his office. We think he's heading home. He'll know where Lexi is hiding."

Turning to SWAT Commander Harrison, Jansen said, "Jed Miller is due here any minute. Let's open a path for him to enter, then close our units behind him."

"On it," Harrison said. He pulled out the wireless mic clipped to his shoulder and relayed the order to Clark.

CHAPTER 30

Lexi

"Just tell me where you're taking me," Meg pleaded.

Lexi said nothing, fearing this wouldn't end well for her and Jed. What was her plan? Her eyes returned to the snow building up along the sides of the roadway as they rose in elevation and moved east into the Cascade Mountains toward the cabin. Meg's whining from the backseat pulled her focus away from the road.

"You're not only a thief, but you can add kidnapping to your list of crimes," said Meg. Lexi looked at her in the rearview mirror, then pulled her focus back to the road.

"Meg," said Lexi. "How did you get in this mess?"

"What you call a mess is the work of my uncle, Dan. He's a greedy bastard."

"You can say that again," said Lexi. "I liked Bruce. He was a straight shooter. I asked him to find me a copy of *The Birds of America*. Once he located it, he gave me a price without haggling and promised it would come on the market within six months. I asked no questions about where he was getting it. I trusted him. I gave him a $200,000 down payment, 10 percent of the $2 million selling price."

"Well, now you know now where the books came from and why they need to go back to the library," said Meg.

"You're a broken record. I paid $4 million for the books. They're mine. I'll never give them up. Once I publish my bird paintings, Audubon's books will be worthless."

"I guess you should know that Mark Larson, the chief of detectives for the Portland Police Bureau, is my fiancé. He will hunt you to the end of the earth."

"That's a valuable piece of information. You'll be a big bargaining chip when Jed and I are planning our escape. If it makes you feel better, we're going to my East Lake cabin. We'll hide out there until Jed comes for me." She knew Jed would have a plan.

A half-hour later, Lexi arrived at the Miller's storage area where they kept a two-person snowmobile, ski clothes, and several locked cabinets with tools and supplies. She used a keypad to open the door, walked in, and turned on the lights and a heater.

"Meg, we're going to change into winter gear and then ride to the cabin. Unless you want to freeze to death, you'll get dressed. The ride into the cabin will take 20 minutes. I'll remove the tape from your hands so you can dress. More important, you'll need both hands to hang on tight during the ride. If you fall off, you'll likely break your neck. I suspect Detective Larson wouldn't appreciate you suffering more injuries. Are you going to cooperate?"

Meg nodded. Lexi removed the tape binding Meg's hands and instructed her to suit up and hurry. "One more thing, Meg. I have no intention of hurting you. You're an innocent bystander. I just need your presence until Jed comes, and then you can go free."

While Meg finished dressing in a snowsuit, gloves, hat, and goggles, Lexi fired up the snowmobile. She locked up three of the four *Birds of America* folios in a large closet in the shed, then placed the fourth book in a waterproof bag and tied it to the snowmobile. Next, she packed a rifle, Jed's BB gun, and several handguns. The cabin was stocked with enough personal items, food, water, and fuel for heat and cooking for three months. Cords of wood for the fireplace were stacked neatly along one side of the cabin. A full propane tank powered a heater and stove.

After twenty minutes churning through the powdery snow, Lexi pulled the snowmobile around to the back of the cabin. Lexi took Meg into the cabin, taped her hands again, then fired up the heater and lights. She pulled out her satellite phone and looked for messages from Jed. There were none.

Next, she made two cups of tea, removed the tape from Meg's hands, and gave her a cup. They sipped silently for a few minutes before Meg said, "I had a dream once. I planned to work my way up the ladder to become the director of the Portland library system. I was offered the assistant director's position but had to give it up when Dad suffered a heart attack and needed help at the store."

"How did Dan get tangled in this mess?" Lexi asked.

"Dan, at Dad's request, showed up a month ago to analyze the store's finances. He found what we already knew: that the COVID pandemic and online bookstores had nearly put McQuillan's Books out of business. Then Dad, who was dying from COPD and cancer, asked Dan to help him with his assisted suicide and to take over the negotiations with you for *The Birds of America*. Dan is a snake. I don't care if he dies."

Lexi cringed. "I'm so sorry. I had no idea Bruce was sick. But I believe that choosing the time and place of your death is far better than suffering a slow, painful death from cancer. I hate the obituaries that say someone battled cancer for years. What's the point?"

"None of that matters," said Lexi. "Right now, I'm going to set up the Audubon book I brought and my paints and work on capturing his style. While I'm painting, you'll need to find something to do. There's no internet or phone service. If you decide to run, you won't get far in the snow or ice on the lake. So, I suggest you find something to read from our bookshelves. If you like novels, there's a good crime thriller, *Bloody Pages*, with a woman detective, on the hunt for two bad guys."

CHAPTER 31

Jed

Jed Miller had been in surgery when word came that someone was locked in his safe room. How the hell had that happened? Hospital security had provided no other details. To keep his focus on his patient, he called out the entry code and instructed hospital security not to interrupt him again. A text message from Lexi he read after surgery didn't explain.

After trying to call Lexi, he logged onto his cellphone location app and confirmed Lexi was near the cabin. The location finder stopped at their storage shed. Beyond that, they had no service, and he wouldn't be able to contact her while she was on the snowmobile ride out there. Once at the cabin, she could text him using a satellite communication device she carried with her anytime she was outdoors alone. He decided to head home to wait for her call.

Jed's stomach clenched as he drove up the hill toward his home and saw a line of police cars and men in jackets emblazoned with FBI on the back. He didn't want to believe all the efforts he and Lexi had taken to disguise the works of the C-14 Foundation and protect its members had failed. Maybe someone had been hurt, and their presence had nothing to do with the C-14 Foundation's activities. Instinctively, he knew better. What had started as a philanthropic organization to protect endangered birds and bird habitats across the globe had turned into an international poaching ring. How did that happen? It wasn't hard to figure.

Wealthy people like him and Lexi and the members of the Red Flock—with money to burn—were forever searching for excitement and new adventures. The Red Flock literally traveled to the ends of the earth to record the rarest of birds for their life lists. They did it often and in luxury. And they didn't mind pouring money into legitimate causes for birding preservation. But, after a while, the line between protecting the ecosystem and helping destroy it blurred.

The Red Flock had given millions to achieve its preservation goals. Then Lexi suggested a step beyond legal: import rare birds going extinct. Why not, she argued. They're going to disappear soon anyway. He remembered her words clearly. "We'll catch them for our enjoyment until they die. Then Jed will taxidermy them, and I'll paint their portraits."

Lexi's plan had an element of selfishness. They would be part of her proposed art masterpiece, combining photos and paintings in a way James Audubon never could have in the early 1800s. While Audubon had to kill dozens of birds for each painting, she would not need to slaughter endangered species to achieve her goal. They would die naturally.

Lexi's dream was dead, Jed thought, as he looked at the car window at the law enforcement presence.

As he pulled up toward the large circular driveway near the front door, an FBI agent held up his hand and signaled for Jed to lower his window. "Identify yourself, please," the agent ordered, his hand resting on his weapon. The agents had been waiting for Jed's arrival.

"I'm Jed Miller. This is my home."

"Please step out of the car," the agent said, pulling his weapon.

"Is that really necessary? I'm not armed."

"Step out of the car," he ordered again, with no "please" attached this time. Jed opened the door and stepped out.

The agent had radioed ahead, and a few seconds later, a half dozen agents with guns drawn filled the driveway, their weapons trained on Miller.

"Put your hands behind your back," another agent ordered. Jed did as he was told, and an agent secured him with handcuffs. A moment later, Perez walked over to Jed.

"Dr. Miller, I am arresting you for violations of U.S. and international laws designed to prevent poaching of endangered species. You will also be charged with conspiracy, along with fellow C-14 Foundation members who took part in this venture." She read him his rights.

"Your wife, Lexicon Anne Miller, will be additionally charged with the theft of art, in this case, *The Birds of America*, protected under the 1970 UNESCO

Convention on the Means of Prohibiting and Preventing the Illicit Import, Export and Transfer of Ownership of Cultural Property."

Jed's head dropped toward his chest, and his shoulders sagged. He took a deep breath, then straightened up. "You're wasting your time going after Lexi or connecting her to the Audubon books. You need to do your homework. Just a week ago, I was outbid trying to buy a copy of *The Birds of America* for $11 million. Lexi subsequently found a rare book dealer to track down another copy for her. It was a legitimate sale."

"Where is Lexi?" Jed demanded. "I want to see her." He knew where she was but wasn't going to let the police know. He needed to get out to the cabin.

"Why don't you tell us where she is," Perez said. "She's not here. She left behind a gunshot victim she locked in your home's safe room. The victim is Dan McQuillan, another co-conspirator."

"Oh, no," said Jed. "What happened?"

"We're piecing that together."

"Where is she?" Jed repeated.

"Don't play coy," said Perez. "On top of the federal and international law violations, your wife will be charged with the murder of Marc Stanfield. If Mr. McQuillan dies, she is looking at a second murder charge."

"What the hell are you talking about?"

"Your wife had an affair with Marc Stanfield, the former curator of the rare book collection at the Portland Central Library. She convinced him to steal the library's copy of *The Birds of America*. Now, he's dead, and the books are missing."

"It can't be true," he said. "Lexi would never cheat on me. There is no way she would have sex with another man to get a copy of the Audubon work." In his heart, though, Jed knew Lexi was capable of anything to achieve her goals. Would she use sex as a weapon? Never, was his first thought. Maybe, was his second thought. He grimaced.

"This is all a big mistake. We've done nothing illegal. In fact, we deserve a medal for our work to protect birds across the planet."

"Dr. Miller, why don't you tell us where your wife has gone?" Perez asked. She ignored his claim of innocence.

Jed was surrounded by FBI agents and police. He decided the only possible escape for Lexi and him was to appear to cooperate and claim innocence.

"We have a cabin on East Lake. You have to cross-country ski or ride a snowmobile this time of year to get there. We keep a snowmobile in a locked storage area a few miles from the cabin. Let me text Lexi and see where she is."

"Where's your phone?" Perez said.

"Left front jacket pocket."

She reached in and pulled it out. "What's the passcode?"

"It's 1414," he said.

Perez opened the phone and saw a message from Lexi. "Don't go home. I'll explain later. Going to the cabin. Cop's girlfriend is with me."

CHAPTER 32

Jansen

1

Perez called Jansen over, gave her Lexi's location, and showed her the message on Jed Miller's phone. "Apparently she's taken Meg McQuillan as a hostage."

"Larson will go crazy when he finds out," said Jansen. "What's our next move?"

"The scene here is under control," Perez said. "My team is collecting evidence, including computers that belong to the Millers and their foundation. Jim and Colin have provided depositions and videos of rare birds to lock down our case. The Millers and their friends should go away for a long time."

"But will they?" Jansen asked. No doubt they'll lawyer up, claiming innocence. We've both watched how money can buy the best lawyers who are experts at bringing the justice system to a grinding halt."

"Sadly, that's the truth," said Perez. "We'll worry about that later. Right now, I need to order out our SWAT helicopter, then have them pick us up and head for the cabin where Lexi is holed up with Meg. I'll alert Deschutes County Sheriff Mary Estes to meet us there, but have her hold back her deputies until we've secured the scene."

Perez's phone rang. She listened, then growled, "We have a SNAFU."

Jansen looked at her, waiting for the bad news.

"Our freakin' helicopter was taken in yesterday for emergency maintenance. The repairs have been completed and the bird is ready to fly. But it can't lift off before it gets FAA clearance. Normally, the process could take hours. I've asked for emergency authorization. I should hear within the hour."

"We don't have one hour to wait," Jansen warned. "Lexi could be long gone while you try to put all this together."

"What's the alternative?" Perez asked.

I've got a plan. Let me make a call, and I'll run it by you."

She stepped away and called Portland Police Bureau's chief pilot, Lt. Bob James, to discuss her idea. He thought about it for a minute and agreed to help. Jansen hung up and explained the plan to Perez.

"I like it," said Perez. "Good luck. See you there. Wait for our back up team. We'll get there as soon as possible."

2

"Larson, grab your snow gear and meet me at the air support unit hangar ASAP," Jansen said when he picked up the phone. "We're going after Lexi Miller, who's holed up in a cabin at East Lake. Bob James will take us up and drop us near the cabin." She delayed talking about Meg. She needed him to focus on the challenge ahead.

"Wait a minute, Jansen. What the hell do you mean drop us in?"

"Do you recall a few summers ago when we went skydiving in the Gorge as a team-building exercise for the Bureau?"

"Hell yes, I remember. I'm terrified of heights. Jumping out of the plane nearly made me shit my pants."

"Well, pull on your diapers," she said. "We'll dive from the plane at 10,000 feet and glide to the shore. We'll be in the air for about 30 seconds before landing. Hopefully, we'll avoid the lake surface. We don't want to crash through the ice."

"We're parachuting onto a frozen lake?" Larson said, his voice a squeak.

"Don't be a pussy," Jansen gibed. "If I can do it, you can, too. See you at the airport. And, there is one more thing you need to know. Lexi Miller is holding Meg hostage."

Larson was suddenly speechless. He was nervous about the drop until he thought about Meg. She was in danger and he no choice. He had to go.

"What are we waiting for?" asked Larson, jumping out of his chair. "I'll be there as fast as I can."

Thirty minutes later, Larson and Jansen were loading ski gear and weapons into the plane.

"Let me check your parachutes," said Sgt. James.

"Is this really necessary, Jansen?" Larson asked. "Wouldn't it be safer for the FBI to do their thing rather than rush in like stormtroopers?"

"You're not wimping on me," said Jansen. They both checked their service weapons and snapped them into their holsters. AR-15 rifles had been disassembled and strapped to their chests. A few minutes later, they were airborne. Sooner than they expected, they were approaching the target.

"James, after we drop, call and tell Perez we're on the ground assessing the situation. Let her know that I have a satellite communicator. I'll text her our GPS coordinates and any relevant tactical information. Larson and I don't want to get killed when her team arrives and sees two people in snowsuits emerging from the woods with guns." He gave her a thumb up. "Time to go," he said. "Good luck."

Without hesitation, Jansen smiled at Larson, pushed open her door, and jumped. Seconds later, her chute opened, breaking her free-fall. As she drifted down, she pulled on the chute lines to steer toward an area with cover about 100 yards from the cabin.

Larson closed his eyes. He couldn't do it. But what was the alternative? Once again, Meg came into focus: his future wife and mother of his children was in jeopardy.

James tapped Larson on the top of his helmet to get his attention. Larson opened his eyes and shook his head as if he had changed his mind. James recognized the hesitation, typical of amateur divers. James nodded, ignored the plea, and mouthed, "Go. Now."

Larson took a deep breath, pushed out into crystal clear blue sky, and began his plunge. He kept his eyes closed until he felt the jerk of his chute opening. As he drifted toward the lake's surface, his fear turned into awe. A white wonderland of ice and snow-covered pines spread out beneath him. His chute fluttered lightly in the rushing air, the sound like a bird's flapping wings. Except for a slight buzzing from the retreating drop plane's engines, the world was dead calm. Then shots rang out, echoing across the empty space.

Several bullets shredded Larson's chute, the speed of his descent suddenly out of control like a runaway train. Seconds later, he slammed down hard, his knee buckling on impact. He screamed as a lower leg bone hit with a loud crack.

Jansen had already touched down and was pulling in her chute when she heard the shots. She looked up and saw Larson coming down fast, then slamming into the ground. She raced to Larson's crumpled form and pulled in his chute. More shots rang out.

From the cabin, Lexi's voice echoed across the ice. "Don't come any closer, Detective Jansen. You've seen me at the firing range, so you know I'm a damn good shot. I suggest you drop your weapons and walk toward me. It's the only way everyone is getting out of here alive."

"Lexi, it's over," said Jansen. "We know you're holding Meg McQuillan. You need to let her go. We know Dan killed Marc Stanfield, so you're off the hook for a murder charge, but you and Jed are going away for bird poaching. The theft of Audubon's bird paintings will add another federal charge. Jed is already in custody. You've got no place to go. Don't make it worse by hurting Meg."

"What's the matter with you?" Larson hissed. "Telling Lexi that she's trapped with no way out could be a death sentence for Meg." Jansen looked at Larson but said nothing.

"One place I'm not going is to jail," Lexi said, her voice wavering. Jansen could tell Lexi's bravado was melting. Lexi stepped out of the cabin's front door and aimed in the direction of Jansen's voice. Once more, Lexi attempted to flush Jansen out of the bushes with several shots. Jansen remained prone in the snow, invisible in her pure white suit and matching hood. Lexi stepped back into the cabin but didn't close the door.

Jansen used Lexi's retreat to assemble her rifle, then formed a tripod with her elbows and waited for Lexi to return to the porch. When Lexi swung around the door and aimed in her direction for another volley of shots, Jansen pulled the trigger, the bullet exploding the wood door frame near Lexi. A scream followed the shot, "You bitch. I'm going to kill you."

Instead of retreating, Lexi yelled, "I'm going to get you," before firing a fusillade of high-powered bullets that struck all around Jansen. One of them ripped through her snowsuit, grazing her shoulder. A moment later, Jansen heard a helicopter overhead. She looked up and saw a heavily armed FBI tactical team with rifles trained on Lexi.

Over a loudspeaker in the air from above came a voice familiar to Lexi. "This is Jed, Babe. Don't shoot. I'm coming to get you. Everything is okay."

CHAPTER 33

Jed

1

Lexi looked up, rifle in her hands, waiting for her husband to appear.

"Jed, I knew you would come to save me," she mouthed, her words drowned out by the rotors.

"Miller, tell your wife to drop that gun, or she'll be killed. I can't let her wave around a high-powered rifle that could bring down this helicopter, killing all of us."

"Listen, Agent Perez, we may have done some things you consider illegal, but none of those alleged crimes call for the death penalty, even if they were true. Unless you set this helicopter down and let me talk to Lexi, you can expect a bloodbath. She's a big game hunter and sharpshooter with a temper. She doesn't like being backed into a corner. And you're right. We're all going down if she fires at this helicopter and hits the engine."

Perez ordered her pilot to set down on the shore.

"Take off the handcuffs and let me talk to her," said Jed. "She'll put down her weapon and come along quietly. As you can see, she's not pointing the gun at us."

"You've forgotten one important detail," said Perez. "Your wife has taken Meg McQuillan hostage. If McQuillan is killed or injured, a kidnapping conviction could land Lexi on Death Row."

Perez knew it would be risky to allow Lexi Miller to stand in the open with a high-powered rifle that could kill her entire crew. But she decided she would rather de-escalate than lose lives over the theft of artwork. "Stand ready, but don't fire until I give the order," Perez told the tactical team, speaking into her headset.

"Move slowly when you get out. If Lexi aims it at us, all bets are off. Let her know that she needs to send out Meg McQuillan. And you've got five minutes to convince her to surrender."

"I understand," said Jed.

Uncuffed, Jed slid out of his seat and onto the ground, then ran to Lexi and hugged her while talking into her ear. Finally, they walked toward the cabin, holding hands. She continued to hold the rifle, but was holding it loosely, pointed at the ground.

"What the hell are they doing?" Perez yelled. "Heads up, guys. We'll do everything we can to de-escalate and get everybody home safely but prepare yourselves for a fight." Perez had made a judgment call, and it was a bad one. She'd screwed up by allowing Jed Miller and Lexi to return to the cabin armed.

Over a loudspeaker, Perez yelled, "Send out your hostage, then come out with your hands up. Leave your guns in the cabin."

2

"You heard the woman. You need to let me go," said Meg, who Lexi had tied up again.

"She's right," said Jed.

"What are you saying?" asked Lexi.

"Come and sit," said Jed, patting the sofa seat.

Meg decided to stay quiet. She felt that Jed's next words could seal their fate.

Jed explained why resistance was futile: possession of rare birds, Dan McQuillan's gunshot, Meg McQuillan being held captive, and the conspiracy to steal Audubon's paintings added up to a life sentence in prison.

"My career as a doctor and a heart surgery is over. A felony conviction will certainly result in the revocation of my medical license."

"It was all my fault," said Lexi, crying. "I've been so damn selfish and greedy. I let my obsession with Audubon's work destroy the dream life we had created. So now we've lost everything."

"Come here," he said, pulling her close. He kissed her and said, "I love you. It was *our* obsession. We both let it get out of control."

Lexi brightened.

"It's time for a celebration," said Lexi. "I brought our costumes. We'll can share it with the world, sans the sex."

Meg felt a chill snake down her spine. What kind of celebration? What could they possibly celebrate when a lengthy jail term was in their future? What did she mean by their 'last' celebration?

Jed got up, walked behind Meg, and untied her. "You're free to go," he said.

Meg rubbed her wrists, looked at Jed and Lexi, and said, "Giving up will be a lot easier than forcing a standoff with police if that's what you're planning."

"Nope," said Jed. "There will be no standoff. Tell the FBI we'll be out in a few minutes. We won't be armed, so tell them not to shoot."

Meg asked no more questions. Instead, she opened the front door and walked out onto the porch. Her chilled breath and bright sunlight temporarily obscured the scene before her. When her vision cleared, she saw a group of armed men and women aiming at her.

Meg dropped to her knees in the snow, put her hands up, and pleaded, "Don't shoot me." An armed FBI agent ran over to her, grabbed her by the arm, and pulled her behind the helicopter, out of the line of fire. Coming from Meg's left was Kim Jansen, the sleeve of her snowsuit stained with blood. Holding on to Jansen was a hobbling Mark Larson.

"Mark," Meg cried out and ran to him. "What happened?"

Before Larson could answer, Betty Perez saw the cabin door open, and two masked figures emerge, dressed in costumes covered with red bird feathers.

The costumed figures sauntered onto the ice and faced one another.

"Today, you will witness a private love ritual we have performed hundreds of times. It is a celebration of a standoff—one that took place when I was a teenager," said the voice coming from the taller masked bird. The voice obviously belonged to Jed Miller. No doubt the other red bird was Lexi.

Jed told the story of how he killed the cardinal, his obsession with the number 14, and why he became a heart surgeon.

"This is bizarre," Perez said into her microphone for her team to hear. "Put those two in your sights, but don't fire." Jed continued with his story.

Perez and her team were mesmerized, even as they held their fingers pressed to the triggers, ready to shoot, like Jed did all those years before he fired and killed the bird.

"My heart to your heart," said Jed, pressing her hand to Lexi's chest.

"My heart to yours," said Lexi, putting her hand over his heart.

In unison, Lexi and Jed said, "The heart and soul are one. We share the same heart and the same soul. Today, we are one."

Lexi's back was to the group, so they didn't see her pull a .357-magnum pistol from under her costume and fire point blank into Jed's chest. He wobbled, held out his arms like the dying cardinal he had mortally wounded, spun around, and fell onto the ice, looking up at the sky. Lexi fell to her knees. She gazed into his fading blue eyes, then he was dead.

"Goodbye, my love," she said. Lexi stood with the gun hanging at her side.

Before Perez could yell stop, Lexi turned the pistol and shot herself in the chest.

Perez and her team raced to the bodies, their guns still out. Jed and Lexi appeared to be holding hands. Blood flowed onto the ice beneath them.

After a few moments of stunned silence, Perez ordered her team to secure the crime scene.

"Larson, we've got a medic on board," said Perez. "She'll escort you to the hospital while I stay behind to coordinate the evidence collection with the sheriff's department. "

Perez herded Jansen, Larson, and Meg to the helicopter, along with the medic, and gave the pilot instructions to fly them straight to the medical center at OHSU.

The pilot took off with the four belted in and headsets in place. Before heading to the hospital in Portland, the pilot circled overhead, giving them a clear view of the scene below. Sprawled on the ice were two figures dressed in red with bird masks. They appeared to be reaching for one another, linked by the blood covering the ice. FBI agents stood in a perfect circle around them, taking in the odd sight.

"Lexi wanted to be an artist revered for her brilliance," said Jansen over the headset. "The red against the snowy background couldn't be a more perfect picture."

CHAPTER 34

The Aftermath

At the beginning of this book, I revealed my characters' motivations. I promised to give you the answers to the questions I posed at the beginning of this novel.

Here's my perspective. Yours may differ. Just because I created the characters doesn't mean my interpretation is the correct one. It's just the one I chose as I found my story at its end.

Heart Surgeon Jed Miller wanted to be an eagle among sparrows - some might say he is now soaring with the winds.

Artist Lexi Miller wanted to defy her critics. The final scene wasn't the picture she imagined. But the death scene of two red-robed bodies reaching out to one another on the snow-covered lake was its own masterpiece.

Bookman Bruce McQuillan wanted to leave a legacy. He tried. With death approaching and his legacy a dying bookstore, he went against his code of ethics by conspiring to sell the Portland library's copy of *The Birds of America* on the black market. The sale of McQuillan's Books would be its own legacy.

Meg wanted out of her dreary life selling bags of used books. Her wish came true. She closed McQuillan's Books, sold the store's collection of rare books and magazines, and used the cash to move to a smaller, more modern store with affordable rent and a new generation of customers. She cherry-picked titles from McQuillan's for the new location and gave it a new name and focus. She called it Meg's Book Cafe. Customers loved it— a clean, well-lighted place that allowed them to drink coffee, eat muffins, and read their favorite books. Sales soared, and her grandfather's dream of generations of McQuillan booksellers lived on. Her eye healed and her vision cleared. She and Mark bought a copy of the *Cyclops* movie and played it whenever they needed a good laugh.

Chief Detective Mark Larson wanted love. So, he married Meg, quit his job as chief detective, and worked with her in the new bookstore.

Uncle Dan McQuillan got the inheritance he thought he deserved. He apologized to Meg for his greediness over the Audubon book deal. She accepted his apology. A week later, sepsis from his stomach wound ended his life, forever hiding the secret that Bruce McQuillan had killed Marc Stanfield.

Mark Stanfield wanted to save his family. Unfortunately, his family couldn't keep what was left of the down payment he had received from Lexi Miller and couldn't afford to keep their house. However, its sale generated enough savings to pay college tuition for Stanfield's daughter.

Colin Byrne wanted redemption. For the help he gave the FBI in bringing down the C-14 Foundation poaching ring, the judge who had sentenced him to a year in jail and five years of probation ended the probation. As CEO of Byrne Vineyards, he slowly regained his reputation as a vintner who made excellent wines. Although released from his probation agreement, he continued to give speeches about the intergenerational violence and child abuse that had earlier landed him in prison.

Veterinarian Jim Briggs wanted a new career. He got it. Although the C-14 job evaporated with the death of the Millers, Briggs refocused his vet care on birds, taking advantage of America's birding craze. He changed his business name from *Have Paws—Will Travel* to *Have Wings—Will Fly* with new artwork on his mobile veterinary van. He continued to care for the dogs of the homeless for free near the Portland Train Depot twice a month.

Bill Bowman, curator-director of the Portland Central Library's John Wilson Collections, wanted recognition for his work. The Library Board praised him for helping solve the mystery surrounding the disappearance of the library's copy of *The Birds of America*, restoring prestige to the library. Shortly after the books were returned and were found undamaged, he opened the rare book room for new tours featuring the Audubon books. He also was promoted to assistant library director for the entire county library system.

Detective Kim Jansen wanted justice for the victims. She helped solve the theft and the murder. After Mark Larson resigned, Jansen was offered his job as chief of detectives. She turned it down to remain on what she called 'the front lines of justice.' Loads of paperwork wasn't her wheelhouse. Her grazed arm from Lexi's bullet healed up nicely, adding one more scar to her once flawless body, badges of honor for her bravery in the field. Alice Munson won the job as chief detective and promised to be a thorn in Jansen's ass.

Under a deal with the U.S. Justice Department, members of The Red Flock agreed to a plea bargain of no jail time in exchange for all C-14 Foundation's assets, including $25 million in cash to be used to protect threatened birds species. A third of the money went to the American Bird Conservancy. All records were sealed to protect the reputation of the wealthy individuals who claimed to be unwitting participants in the Miller's scheme to import endangered birds.

The Cherry-Throated Tanager and Orange-Bellied Parrot were shipped home and safely returned to the wild.

Finally, we can't forget Trudy, the Miller's dog. She found a home with Mark and Meg and was a popular attraction at their book cafe. The aging dog made her rounds between customers, collecting treats to the chagrin of the Larsons. In the winter, she enjoyed a prominent spot in the book cafe near a large heater.

ABOUT THE AUTHOR

Photo by Dennis F. Freeze

Bruce Lewis was a crime reporter for several California daily newspapers where he earned six awards for best news and feature writing. Bruce is the author of *Bloody Paws*, winner of a Maxy Award for best mystery novel, and *Blood Pages*, a crime thriller dealing with intergenerational violence and child abuse. *Bloody Feathers*, is book three in *The Kim Jansen Detective* series.

He also wrote the *Master Detective Magazine* cover story, *Bloody Murder in Beautiful Downtown Burbank*. In 2021, he and his wife moved from Northwest Portland to the San Francisco East Bay.

ABOUT THE AUTHOR

NOTE FROM THE AUTHOR

Word-of-mouth is crucial for any author to succeed. If you enjoyed *Bloody Feathers*, please leave a review online—anywhere you are able. Even if it's just a sentence or two. It would make all the difference and would be very much appreciated.

Thanks!
Bruce Lewis

ALSO BY BRUCE LEWIS

BLOODY PAWS
A KIM JANSEN DETECTIVE NOVEL

Questions or comments to: BloodyThrillers@gmail.com

Shortly after losing her husband in a freak accident, Veterinarian Helen Williams is brutally attacked by a group of homeless men and left for dead.

Emotionally raw and physically battered, Williams accepts a job to manage a pet crematory and assist Veterinarian Jim Briggs—her college lover—with his canine mobile care business, including doctoring the dogs of the homeless for free.

As homeless people disappear without a trace and police fear a serial killer is on the loose, Mark Larson and Kim Jansen are assigned to the case. Led astray by confusing clues and personal relationships, they struggle to uncover the truth before the killer takes another life.

BLOODY PAGES
A KIM JANSEN DETECTIVE NOVEL

After discovering the family secret that drove his father to nearly beat him to death as a child—an attack that cost him an eye—a millionaire vintner starts down a path of murderous revenge with Detective Kim Jansen the only person who can stop him. With the lives of two men hanging in the balance and suspects mounting, Jansen is soon caught in a maze of clues with no way out.

We hope you enjoyed reading this title from:

BLACK ROSE

writing™

www.blackrosewriting.com

Subscribe to our mailing list – *The Rosevine* – and receive **FREE** books, daily deals, and stay current with news about upcoming releases and our hottest authors.
Scan the QR code below to sign up.

Already a subscriber? Please accept a sincere thank you for being a fan of Black Rose Writing authors.

View other Black Rose Writing titles at
www.blackrosewriting.com/books and use promo code
PRINT to receive a **20% discount** when purchasing.

9 781685 131517